Cowgirl in Love

COWGIRL IN LOVE

A Hartman Brothers Romance

Jamie Dallas

TULE
PUBLISHING

Cowgirl in Love

Copyright© 2022 Jamie Dallas
Tule Publishing First Printing, January 2022

The Tule Publishing, Inc.

First Publication by Tule Publishing 2022

Cover design by Elizabeth Mackey

ISBN: 978-1-956387-01-8

Dedication

To my daughter.

PROLOGUE

"THE WILL STIPULATES that the three sons shall inherit the ranch and the surrounding property provided you all live on the ranch for one year."

Ty Hartman stared at the lawyer as the older man ran a thin, bony finger along the lines of the will, reading out the stipulations in a monotone, blissfully unaware that he had just hammered a nail through all of Ty's dreams.

There was no way this was real.

He was the one who stuck around the ranch. Colton left. His mom left. *He* stayed.

He was the one who kept it going. The one who kept the animals alive and the fences mended even after his father had given up on everything and fallen into a depression. Beau had laid off all the ranch hands and reduced the herds to nothing. Despite that, he stuck around to make sure what little was left was up and running. And he did it all because this land was his legacy. He wanted to pass it on to his kids, and their kids, and keep it right where it belonged—in the family.

It was his dream to not only carry on the legacy, but to set up his vet practice on the ranch, eventually expanding to the point that he could hire more vets, take on specialty cases, and build a reputation as a cutting-edge operation.

And this was how his father thanked him for sticking around when no one else had? By making him share the ranch with two people who didn't want to be there so that he was at risk of losing it? Colton had walked away a decade ago with no plans to return. Hell, Ty hadn't even known that Jace—a half-brother—existed until two weeks ago. Jace had no knowledge of their legacy and to date had shown no interest.

"Our father is trying to manipulate us, even from the grave, and I'm not falling for this bullshit," Colton snapped. He shoved forward in his chair, gripping the armrests.

Ty barely heard the words over the roar in his ears. He'd thought Beau had changed. That his father had finally acknowledged him. And instead, he passed two-thirds of the ranch to his brothers, who would no doubt want to sell. He knew that Colton was practically counting the seconds until he could get on the next plane out of Montana, and, despite not knowing Jace all that well, there was no denying that Jace looked at his watch more times than was necessary.

Ty shifted in the chair, the old wood and leather creaking under his weight.

"Is there a period of time that we can leave for and not break the will?" Again it was Colton, his voice carrying that tense note he always had when he spoke about their father.

The lawyer glanced over his glasses, taking time to stare at each of them in turn. "You can leave for one month, at most, during this one-year probation period. If you leave for longer than a month, you forfeit your right to the inheritance, and the estate will be donated to the University of Montana's agricultural department."

Ty held his breath as the lawyer glanced back at the document and continued to lay out the rules in the same monotone as before. Essentially, they all three needed to stay on the ranch, or they would lose the property.

The lawyer would stop by intermittently to check on them, and he only lived about a couple miles away, which was not that far in rural terms.

One thing was for certain, there was no way in hell Ty was leaving this ranch. His boots were staying firmly planted in Garnet Valley and the Rocking H land. He was going to follow the rules. However, he wasn't so sure about Colton or Jace. Neither of them wanted to stay on the ranch and both had been pretty clear about it.

Meanwhile, Colton kept throwing out possibilities as to how they could keep the ranch while he returned to California.

He needs cash.

That was the only reason Ty could think of that would cause his brother to want to keep a ranch that had never meant anything to him.

Maybe Jace was in the same boat. He looked just as interested as Colton in leaving as quickly as possible while still holding onto the property.

Ty's gut clenched. If they needed cash, they'd want to sell when the year was up.

But the ranch was Ty's life, his blood. He couldn't lose it.

His brain shifted into overdrive. There had to be a way to fix this. What had his father been thinking, passing the ranch to all three of them, when two of them didn't care? His dad knew Ty's plans and dreams.

And once again, his father completely disregarded them.

"We aren't interested in our legacy. Is there no other alternative?" Colton demanded as soon as he ran out of scenarios where he could leave and still hang onto the property.

That spurred Ty into action. If he didn't say something soon, the ranch would belong to the University of Montana and all three of them would be left with nothing.

"Speak for yourself," Ty snapped, turning on his older brother. "The legacy is ours, and I don't want to throw it away." More than anything, it deserved to be passed down to future generations, even if all that remained were rundown buildings and a pathetically tiny herd of livestock.

"You don't plan to keep the ranch, do you?" Colton's incredulous question was answer enough for Ty. Colton needed cash.

"The ranch is ours, and I don't think we should make any rash decisions about it." He spoke with the same voice he used with panicked clients who brought in their injured animals.

Both brothers stared at him like he had sprouted antlers.

His throat felt tight, too tight, making it impossible to breathe. His heart hammered against his ribs, threatening to break one as it worked overtime to keep oxygen circulating.

It seemed that his heart was as panicked as his brain.

"I'll fight this," Colton hissed at the lawyer, but the barb felt more aimed at Ty than at the lawyer.

Colton clearly wanted to sell.

Ty closed his eyes, feeling sick as his mind whirled in circles trying to figure out how to handle the situation. He had to stop his brothers from breaking the ranch into three parts and selling it—or worse, losing it all together. Their jobs weren't tied to the land. His was. If he lost the ranch, he'd have nowhere to live.

He needed to start saving as soon as possible. Thankfully, he had a year to add to the nest egg he had built up. The trouble was, there was no way he could afford to buy out both brothers. Which meant he needed at least one brother to stick around after the year probation period.

And if he bought out a brother, there was no way he could afford to expand his practice to the ranch. It was like his dad was forcing him to choose—the ranch that was his legacy or the vet practice he had built from scratch.

Ty glanced at the man who was supposedly his eldest brother. The shock of seeing someone who looked like him and Colton still hadn't eased.

Jace's jaw was tense, and he gripped the ends of the armrests in his tight fists. There was no way Jace was going to stick around. He'd lived his whole life unaware of Montana or his legacy. Sure, he was from Texas, but did this guy even know a horse from a cow?

The lawyer finally wrapped up the reading. The second the will was set on the desk, and the lawyer was done, Colton was on his feet and out of the office, moving faster than a herd of cows bolting toward an open gate.

Shit. Ty stared at his brother's retreating back before willing his feet forward.

He still didn't have an idea if either Jace or Colton planned to stick around. They needed to get something sorted between the three of them. Because if even one of them left, the ranch was instantly forfeited.

He needed both men to stick around, including Colton, who would rather cut off an arm than do anything for his father. Hopefully Colton would be willing to stay as a favor for a brother.

Ty pushed out of the chair and chased after his brother. "Colton, we need to hash this out."

"There's nothing to hash out. I'm not sticking around. I can't do this. I have to go back to California."

"Then we lose this ranch," he snapped. His life, sweat, and time were engrained in the lands of the Rocking H. He couldn't lose it. His dreams were centered around this ranch. *His ranch.* "The ranch is our legacy."

"Ha!" Colton whirled around and jabbed him in the chest. "Our legacy? A bitter man lived there and ran it into the ground."

And he was doing everything he could to keep it from falling apart. Once he moved his practice to the ranch, he could dedicate more time and funds to repairing the ranch and restore it to its former glory. He almost, *almost* told Colton.

But he snapped his mouth shut before he could say anything. After all, Colton had left ten years ago. It wasn't like he was that close to his brother anymore. Colton probably thought it was a ridiculous idea to keep the ranch, dream or no dream.

"Look, we all know Dad wasn't the greatest, but that doesn't mean we should throw our history out. William Hartman started the ranch six generations ago. It's ours, well and truly." He was practically pleading with his brother, trying to make him realize just how valuable the ranch was—for all of them. Of him and Jace, Colton would be the one who understood how important the legacy was. He and their dad may have fought, but he'd been raised on the land.

Colton shook his head and pressed his palms against his eyes. "I don't want to deal with this now."

Ty stared at his brother, his neck tense in frustration. "Colton, I have big plans centered around this ranch."

Colton's jaw set as he met Ty's gaze before dropping his head and rubbing at the back of his head.

"Sorry, Ty." The words were barely out of his mouth before Colton hopped into his SUV and backed out of the spot.

"I've got to admit," Jace said as they watched Colton drive off, "I'm with your brother on this. What are we going to do with the ranch? Our lives are elsewhere."

"Mine's not," he said stonily, fury at his father riding him hard.

His life was on the ranch. And it was sifting through his fingers like grains of sand.

There had to be a way to convince his brothers to stick around. He hadn't spent years dealing with Beau to have his dreams go down the drain.

Colton was right about one thing; his dad was an ass. Ty had tried, damn how he tried, to make his relationship with his dad work, but his dad was never happy. Not with anything, or anyone, especially not with him.

His brother was wrong about the legacy, though. Ty was going to make sure it lived on in his name. One way or another, the Rocking H belonged to him.

Chapter One

Four months later

THE SONG BLASTING on the speakers pointed toward the dance floor was classic country George Strait, and honestly, the music was the only thing making this dance tolerable.

Ty Hartman muttered the words to the song under his breath as he wove through the crowd searching for his two brothers who had talked him into coming along only to ditch him the second their women wanted to dance.

It was the first year the Dillon Rodeo Board had decided to have a dance as part of the rodeo weekend, and it appeared to be a huge success, if Ty was any judge. Unfortunately, large crowds, loud music, and drunk people everywhere were not his vibe. He preferred working quietly with animals.

The parking lot outside the arena was blocked off with straw bales and barrels to create the outdoor event space, and the early fall evening air felt even warmer with the press of bodies on the dance floor and milling about.

More than anything, he was ready to head back to his hotel and crash before another big day as one of the rodeo veterinarians. Unfortunately, his two brothers—Jace and Colton—had disappeared over an hour ago, and he hadn't seen them since. For the dozenth time that night, he wished he had insisted on driving himself rather than let Colton talk him into heading over with him and his girlfriend Gus. Despite the fact he hated being at the whim of others, he'd agreed.

Turning slowly on his heel, he scanned the crowd carefully, trying to spot one of his brothers or their significant others. Instead, he ran into Roy Silverman, a successful team roper who Ty had worked with many times on the Montana rodeo circuit.

Ty tucked his thumbs in his pockets and tried to paste on a friendly look despite the fact he'd rather just find his brothers and leave.

"Hey, Ty." Roy shook Ty's hand. "I overheard you talking with Josh about pressure point therapy earlier. He looked pretty up in arms. I wanted to make sure everything was good between you two."

Josh was Roy's team roping partner and his horse had a recent injury. Ty offered to try pressure point therapy on the gelding, but Josh was convinced Ty was peddling some sort of snake oil to try to make a buck off the team roper. The more Ty tried to convince the cowboy otherwise, the more annoyed Josh got until Ty just gave up.

Ty shook his head and took a step back. "Everything is fine. I thought I would offer a service to help out Josh's horse, but it looks like he'd rather just wait and see."

Roy nodded, his mouth pulled tight. "It does sound like a bit of hocus-pocus. Pressure point therapy—that's what you call it, right? Have you had a successful case?"

Reluctantly, he shook his head. "I haven't had an opportunity to try it myself."

"Right. Hey, if you have proof it works and someone to

back it up, let me know. I'll send all my horses your way," Roy said, then added, "Josh's horses as well."

That was the challenge about some of the cowboys around these parts—they always went with the familiar, and something new wasn't readily accepted until they had the proof in front of their eyes.

Nonetheless, he would keep trying. He wrapped up the small talk with Roy and went back in search of his brothers.

However, between the dim lighting and the hundreds of people, it was impossible to spot them in the sea of cowboy hats. He pulled his phone out of his pocket and let out a frustrated snort. So far, no one had responded to his texts that he was ready to head back.

Pressing the pad of his palm against the bridge of his nose, he started searching for someone he knew that wouldn't mind giving him a ride. He gazed through the crowd, scanning for a familiar face, when his eyes landed on her.

His heart slammed to a sudden halt, jolting in his chest so hard, his breath jammed in his throat.

Damn it.

Caught like a deer in headlights, he stopped, rooted in place, unable to look away as Ella James Sanders leaned against a small stack of straw, legs stretched out in front of her. Her long dark hair cascaded in waves to just below her breasts. She tapped her dark boot against the pavement in rhythm with the music. With a lazy grace that defined all her movements, she raised a bottle of beer to her lips and took a long pull as she watched the crowd of people dance.

Even after all these years, his reaction to Ella had not

changed. Hell, it had gotten worse with time.

And he hated it.

Despite his best efforts, despite the fact he no longer wanted anything to do with her, and despite the knowledge she clearly didn't like him for reasons still unknown, his heart shoved away from his ribs and began to pulse wildly.

He had been avoiding her for the past two days—hell, for the entire rodeo season—but since he'd been hired to provide vet services for these rodeo events, and she was the rising barrel racing star of the year, it wasn't a surprise he'd run into her eventually. That didn't make it any easier.

Ella ran her fingers through the long length of her curls, her silky hair easing through her fingers before bouncing back into place.

Closing his eyes, he took a deep breath. Ella had been clear she wanted nothing to do with him the last time they spoke. And after being rejected twice, the feeling was mutual. He wasn't going to go out on a limb for her again.

She hadn't seen him yet, so there was no reason he couldn't back away and pretend he never saw her. She'd be none the wiser.

Stepping back, he pulled his gaze away. Hard to believe that she'd been his high school crush. Despite the bad blood between their fathers, he always felt drawn to her. Her determination to come out on top at rodeos, the no-nonsense way she handled everything from cattle drives to conversations, and the way she laughed right after giving one of her rare smiles drew him to her.

After a year of crushing on her, he had decided that asking

her to junior prom was the best way to let her know his feelings. Of course he couldn't just ask her, he wanted this prom proposal to be special. Weeks went into planning it— where to do it, how to ask, the music he would play. While he wasn't one for grand gestures or big to-dos, as a junior in high school with oversized feelings and a planet-sized crush, he felt the only way to win her over was a big display.

Clearly Ella had not felt the same way. Because after blasting "Hooked on a Feeling" from the stadium loudspeakers and having his dog trot out with a sign that he had decorated himself asking her to prom as he got down on one knee holding a bouquet of flowers, she very swiftly and cleanly cut him down in front of his friends and half the school.

Talk about a wake-up call.

The dance music switched from George Strait to a top hit that Ty didn't know the name of. The pop-country beat blared from the nearby speaker as he took a step back and turned away before Ella could spot him. However, before he could stop himself, a moment of weakness took over. Turning back, he took her in once more.

And stopped dead in his tracks.

Or rather it was the two men walking toward her that stopped him. Ty narrowed his eyes as Jeff Parker and his sidekick Aaron Roberts headed for Ella.

Years ago, he and Jeff had been friends. Small towns and travel to junior rodeo then high school rodeo threw the two of them together frequently, and from childhood through high school, Ty had chosen to turn a blind eye to the fact Jeff never heard the word "no" growing up, hoping Jeff would end up a decent human being. Unfortunately, he ended up very much like his entitled, cheating father and Ty had cut ties a few years ago.

The two ambled over to Ella with a loose-limbed stagger that sent up warning flags.

Instinct kept him anchored in place as Ella's laid-back posture became rigid as the men approached.

Where were her friends? Ella had always been independent, even in high school. However, he knew she was rarely on her own these days since becoming a top barrel racer in the Montana circuit.

He didn't approach yet. For all he knew, the two guys were going to say hi and then disappear into the night. Or veer in another direction at the last minute.

As though sensing her gaze on him, Ella turned toward him, and her eyes met his.

His breath caught in his throat, and despite the distance between them, a slow sizzle of heat burned through him.

But as Jeff and Aaron closed in on her, her expression shifted from surprised to vulnerable. Before Ty could think twice, he was moving toward her with grim determination. After their past encounters, Ella may not be his favorite person in the world, and he sure as heck wasn't hers, but there was no way in hell he was going to leave her to defend herself with these guys.

Jeff leaned against the straw bales, blocking her exit on one side. Aaron situated himself right in front of her. The two men moved in a way that confirmed to Ty the amount of alcohol they had consumed.

He couldn't get to her fast enough. The second he was

close enough for her—and these two assholes—to hear him over the music, he called out her name.

Her head jerked in his direction, and there was no way he was imagining the relief on her face. Ella wrapped an arm over her chest and hooked her fingers around the strap of her simple black tank, as though locking a shield into place. "It's good to see you."

Yep, if Ella was happy to see him, she was definitely uncomfortable.

"I was looking for my brothers and spotted you. Thought I'd say hi." He gestured at the two men scowling at him. "Wanted to make sure everything was good."

"Everything is fine," Jeff slurred, leaning heavily against the straw bales and fixing Ella with a leering gaze that made Ty clench his hands into hard fists. "Just saying hi to Ella here."

His presence must have given her courage because Ella pulled her shoulders back. "These two were just saying hi and continuing on their way."

"Ella, honey. Don't be like that." Jeff pushed away from the stack of straw and farther into her space. "You know, Lindsey and I broke up. You and I—"

Ella cringed, the movement so miniscule the two men probably didn't notice, but it was just enough that Ty's anger flared hot.

"I don't think so," he snapped, shoving a hand hard against the other man's chest and inserting himself between them and Ella. "The lady asked you to go. I think it's time to go."

"Just one dance first," Jeff crooned. He reached around Ty to hold out his hand.

Even with his back to her, Ty could feel her recoil. "No way, Jeff. I made that mistake with you once before. It's never going to happen again."

He almost took his eyes off Jeff. This happened once before? That was news to Ty, and pretty surprising. Especially considering Jeff had been dating Lindsey for years.

Jeff's scowled deepened as he lunged for her hand. "You act all high and mighty for someone whose family is trash—"

Ty heard Ella's sharp intake of breath, and his restraint begun to fray. Ella Sanders may have grown up on the wrong side of town, but she was not trash. Yes, her family had struggled at times, but that didn't make the Sanders family less than Jeff and his kind in any way.

"It's time to move on," Ty growled. He slammed his hand down onto Jeff's shoulder, pressing hard against the other man's clavicle and digging his thumb under Jeff's collarbone.

Jeff's eyes narrowed but he flinched from Ty's grip.

Sure there were two of them, but Ty had them both in height and build. And there was no way Jeff had forgotten the time that Ty bested him in high school when he'd gotten too handsy with Ty's then-girlfriend.

"Go away, Jeff." Ella's voice was surprisingly firm. "You're drunk, and I'm not interested in dancing with you. Now or ever."

"She doesn't want to dance with you," Ty repeated, driving the point home.

Jeff looked ready to argue, but Ty shot him another hard look, and the other cowboy relented. Aaron, who hadn't spoken a word the entire time, preferring to leer at Ella, jerked his head.

"Whatever, dude." Jeff gave one last slimy look, then he and Aaron turned away. "She isn't worth it anyway."

Ty kept his eyes on them until the two men were out of site. Their path was more of a zigzag than a straight line as they disappeared into the crowd.

Once he was certain the two were not returning, he faced Ella. Part of him wanted to look her over, pull her close, and make sure she was okay. However, he knew better. Ella had barriers up when it came to him, and he wasn't willing to cross them.

Unfortunately, he couldn't think of what to say to ease the situation.

"The dude doesn't like no," he offered.

Ella rolled her eyes and grabbed the jacket and purse sitting on the straw stack behind her. "Apparently not. I was thrilled when he left Garnet Valley, but I still see him at rodeos." She motioned in the direction the two men had left. "My past lack of judgment seems to haunt me when it comes to that one."

He must have done a bad job hiding his surprise because Ella's frown deepened into a scowl.

Something had happened with her and Jeff. He didn't know what it was, but it was clear Jeff felt she owed him in some way. A curl of anger on her behalf twisted through him.

Grabbing a lock of dark hair, she wound it, and then unwound it, from her finger.

"Where are your friends?" There was no way he was leaving her until he was certain that she was safe.

Ella dropped the curl. "I'm waiting for Jordan to grab

drinks while I watch our stuff." She looked around, as though waiting for Jordan to appear. A group of people passed by, waving at Ella and saying hi. Ella waved back as though she hadn't been harassed or that she was hanging out with a man she'd coldly rejected for the second time six months ago. "I'm sure she'll be here shortly. You don't have to stick around."

He wasn't leaving her on her own. Not until he knew for sure those two assholes weren't returning and that she was with her friend.

"You're getting popular these days," Ty said, trying for easy conversation.

"I think that's what winning does for a woman," she drawled, staring out at the crowds. Her eyes never landed on him. "Everyone seems to like a winner."

There was no missing the barb in her voice. So much for an easy conversation.

"You were a winner before you started the pro circuit," he muttered.

"Right," Ella said, the tension evident in her reply. "I'm sure that's what you and the rest of the town think... Oh, there's Jordan. Thank god."

With that, the conversation dried up. Drier than a creek bed in September after the snowpack had melted away.

Clearly, she wanted him to walk away. Now.

He stayed firmly rooted in place.

Maybe it was the evening air. Maybe it was the one beer he had to make this dance more tolerable. Or maybe it was the fact he wanted to see her walk off with Jordan, so he knew she was in good hands.

Or maybe he was a damn fool that couldn't seem to walk away from her. Despite the fact she made her feelings clear— twice.

"That line took forever," Jordan said, a little breathlessly. She carried a bottle of water and a beer. She handed the water to Ella. "Hey, Ty. Fancy seeing you here, cowboy."

He nodded hello but kept his eyes on Ella.

As though sensing the mood, Jordan's gaze quickly went between them. "Is everything okay?"

Ella scrunched her nose but nodded. "Fine. Just fine. But if it's good by you, I'm ready to head back."

Jordan cocked her head to the side but didn't question Ella's request.

"I guess I'm tired as well." Jordan held her Bud Light out to Ty. "Beer?"

Bud Light wasn't his favorite, but he took it without question.

"I won't keep you then," Ella said, lifting her dark brows. She bit her lip, worrying it between her teeth as though she had more to add. Just when he thought she was going to say something else, she lifted her hand in an awkward wave before following her friend to the parking lot.

He watched her leave, telling himself he wanted to make sure she was safe the entire time.

"Ty," a familiar voice called out as Ella and Jordan disappeared behind a row of trucks.

He closed his eyes, uncertain if he was annoyed or grateful. Either way, at least one of his brothers finally found him.

Colton threw an arm around his shoulders. "Was that Ella

Sanders I saw you talking to?"

Ty ran his hand over his face and suppressed a groan. The last person he wanted to talk to about Ella was his happily paired off brother.

"It's not what you think," he said quietly, pulling away from Colton's arm. Ella had proven time and again she wanted nothing to do with him, which was why he usually tried to avoid her. It was the easiest solution. "Look, I'm ready to head back if that works for you guys."

He had a long day ahead of him, and despite the fact he should stay away, he knew he'd find her tomorrow. The least he could do was make sure she was okay and that she and Jordan got home safe.

After that, he could go back to avoiding her.

"IT'S ALMOST TIME, Red." Ella leaned against her horse and took a deep breath. Her nerves were already performing their funny little dances in her belly, but this time, they had an extra punch with each jump and twist.

Considering that she and Jordan were staying at a motel only five minutes away, she'd had a heck of a time getting to the fairgrounds. She'd barely slept after last night's events at the dance. Every time she closed her eyes, Ty coming to her rescue floated to her mind. Even after she had shut him down only a few months earlier, he'd still been protective of her.

Why?

When sleep finally overtook her, it was in the wee hours of

the morning, and she ended up sleeping past her alarm. In her hurry to get out the door, she left her wallet in the room. After turning around to retrieve it, her truck got a flat tire before she could pull into the worn hotel parking lot. At least she had a spare tire and a lot of experience changing them, but it still made her an hour late to the fairgrounds.

She was sweating by the time she got her horse from the stall she had leased for the night.

Bad things happen in threes.

At least that's what her elderly neighbor, Ms. Minna, would say when things weren't going her way. Did sleeping in count as a bad thing?

She hoped so.

Red, her well-muscled sorrel mare, leaned slightly against her as Ella forced the superstitious thought from her mind. Closing her eyes, she mentally played out the pending run.

"We need to make this run count." Ella gave her horse a loving pat on the shoulder. This was one of the last rodeos of the season, and she and Red were right on the cusp of making it to the National Finals Rodeo. She had been neck-in-neck with Lindsey Whitmore all season, but Ella had just recently pulled ahead in the standings.

If everything went well, she'd finally have enough money to buy a small ranch and start her dream of training barrel horses. Then she could prove she wasn't some poor soul who grew up on the wrong side of town.

The announcer's energetic voice echoed over the fairgrounds calling out the team roping. The crowd was getting worked up as the summer sun dipped behind the towering mountains and the temperature began to cool. Barrel racing was up next, and she needed a perfect run.

She could do it. After deciding to go pro this year, she and Red exploded onto the scene, placing in one rodeo after another. Now they were *expected* to win.

The success was thrilling. She had saved enough to buy a new trailer a couple months ago. Well, new to her. It was used but better than the rusted one she'd been hauling around for years.

More importantly, her dream goal to buy a small ranch to train barrel horses was finally within reach.

Ella ran her hand over her mare's neck, the nerves starting to take hold.

Unfortunately, the more wins she stacked up and the closer she came to her goal, the more pressure she felt to perform. She needed to succeed. Had to win. That sickening, nauseous feeling she got before every race was now creeping into her stomach, making her joints weak, and her head swim.

Arf arf arf! A blue-speckled puppy in the bed of the giant silver pickup parked next to her trailer yapped energetically at whatever caught its attention—people, its tail, the butterfly in the breeze.

Everyone who passed by thought the little pup was cuter than all get out. Red, however, had a much different opinion.

The horse flicked her ears back and forth as Ella tacked up, going through the motions as she tried to push back the numbness flooding her limbs.

"Knock it off, girl," Ella grumbled as she bent to strap the blue sport boots around her horse's delicate lower limbs. Before a race, it didn't take much to make her whip-fast horse antsy. This puppy seemed to be the excuse her horse needed to get worked up.

Red snorted but held still long enough to let out a big sigh, giving Ella time to strap on all four boots. The horse's delicate ears, one of Red's only pretty features, continued to pivot back and forth.

Her best friend Jordan was in the tack room, handing over equipment as Ella finished saddling up.

"I'm going to grab something to eat," her friend said, motioning in the direction of the food stands once Red was tacked up. "Do you want anything? It's on me."

"I'm good," Ella said. Eating right before a race didn't mix with her nerves. There was a PB and J sandwich stashed in her cooler for after the race—a cheaper alternative to the rodeo burger since she was saving every dollar earned for a down payment. She dreamed of the day she no longer needed to drive to the local arena in order to work out with Red.

"Alright." Jordan stepped out of the tack room. "In case I don't get back before you take off, good luck with the race. You and Red will kill it."

As if aware someone was talking about her, Red turned her narrow, anvil-shaped head to look at them.

"You're going to Vegas this year, girl," Jordan said, giving Red a pat, and then Ella a quick squeeze. "Don't forget I have to take off right after your run, but I'll see you back in Garnet Valley."

Ella returned the hug. Jordan had been her best friend for years. Her family had lent her a barrel horse during high school rodeo when her dad had to sell hers to the Hartmans; an issue that still ate at her. "Thanks for coming! I'll see you soon."

A few people called hello as Ella grabbed a long-sleeved shirt hanging in the backseat of her truck. She waved back before jumping into the tack room to change.

That was the biggest change from high school rodeo. Once she started winning, everyone became friendlier. It was as though no one had ever judged her for her borrowed horse, faded clothes, or the fact that she was just a touch too thin. No one seemed to care anymore that she grew up in a trailer and had a father who couldn't keep a job.

Even Ty, who had played the prom prank on her in high school, was friendlier now that she was a top barrel racer. While she had been flattered when he approached her at the bar a few months ago, she knew better than to fall for someone like Ty. She had already been burned once, and that was enough.

She tucked her shirt into the waistband of her jeans and grabbed her makeup bag.

It was time to get her head into the game.

Pulling out a red lipstick, she ran the color over her lips and checked her reflection in the trailer mirror. Pushing her dark curls over her shoulders, she pulled her lucky cowgirl hat low over her head. Her cowgirl battle armor in place, she grabbed her bridle and left the tack room.

"Ella?" The rugged voice stopped her in her tracks, and a different kind of nerves washed over her.

Her mouth went dry. Drier than the dirt under her feet from the overly hot day and the thousands of boots and hooves that stamped it to dust.

She would recognize that voice anywhere. The way her body flushed, heating slowly from her core to her extremities, was enough to tell her who it was.

Slowly she turned around to face the one man she always noticed, even when she didn't want to.

He stood there, thumbs tucked in the front pockets of his worn jeans, looking like every bit of sin imaginable. Ty Hartman was the chocolate desert she craved and still denied herself from having a taste.

Maybe, just maybe, she could have forgiven him for trying to pull a prom prank on her their junior year of high school, but there was no way she'd ever trust another handsome, privileged cowboy from Garnet Valley. Not after Jeff, and Ty and Jeff had been friends for years.

He protected you last night, the little voice in her head reminded her.

But that didn't change the fact that the Jeffs and Tys grew up in a different world than she did. They inherited ranches and always had the best horses. She had to pull together a few hundred to buy the ugliest horse at a nearby ranch to train for rodeo. She'd only lucked out when Red turned out to be a winner.

And if Jeff thought she was trash, there was no doubt Ty thought the same thing. Ty's father always seemed to look down on her family, even as he hired them as extra hands.

Even though she was the rising rodeo star of Montana, she would always be from the wrong side of town. And, as her dad pointed out, they would never be good enough in the eyes of people who simply inherited ranches.

"I didn't expect to see you here," she said lightly. She turned back to her horse, her pulse stuttering as she heard the crunch of sand as Ty moved closer.

Red snorted as though even the horse didn't believe her lie. Everyone knew the sexy vet was contracted with the local rodeos in the area in case something went wrong with any of the animals. And for some reason, there were plenty of cowgirls who seemed to find the privileged vet attractive. Some even planned their circuits around his schedule.

She, on the other hand, had better things to do with her time than to deal with men who only wanted her while she was at the top of her game.

Ty leaned against the trailer, pressing his shoulder into the stainless-steel side as though he didn't plan to move until they talked. "Someone told me you had a flat tire this morning. I wanted to make sure you were alright."

She lifted her brow at him. "I'm fine. I'm capable of taking care of myself, thank you."

Ty glanced down at her tires and kicked one with the pointed toe of his boot.

She gritted her teeth. "They aren't bald, if that's what you're checking."

"Just neighborly concern." Ty crossed his arms. The movement flexed the muscles in his chest, and of course the man had the top few buttons of his shirt undone. "I wanted to make sure you got back okay after last night."

Pressing her lips together, Ella forced her gaze back up to his. The man's eyes were brighter than the summer sky, and the fact that she even noticed rankled.

She placed a hand on Red's neck. "I'm good. Just happy that Jeff moved on."

Ty's assessing gaze didn't leave her face.

"I'm fine," she repeated. Though be honest, she had been relieved to see Ty last night. It wasn't that she expected Jeff to try anything, not in the middle of a crowded dance, but she hated that Jeff thought she'd come crawling back now that he and Lindsey broke up.

Ty had put a quick end to that.

And she was grateful for that. Which was a new feeling in terms of how she felt about Ty.

"You know, if anything ever comes up, you can call." Ty snapped his mouth shut the second the words were out. Like he couldn't believe he just offered for her to reach out.

Not that it mattered. She never would. The last thing she needed was a Hartman to come to her rescue. Her father got burned by that once, and the experience was enough for her to learn her lesson about the Hartmans' generosity.

Her hand clenched in Red's mane. "I don't have your number."

"I'm happy to give it to you."

"I'll search for it on the web when I need it." In other words, thanks but no thanks.

Ty didn't seem to be taking the hint. His gaze didn't move as she busied herself, checking her cinch for the fifth time.

"What?" she asked after a few long seconds.

Ty shook his head. "I just—" He ran a hand through his hair, mussing up the dark locks. "Never mind."

Now she was intrigued.

Warning, a small voice in the back of her mind whispered. Finding Ty interesting was not a path she wanted to wander down.

Ty let out a breath and ran a hand along Red's nose. The horse nickered softly, pressing her muzzle into Ty's palm.

Ella glared at her horse.

Traitor.

"I need to warm up." Her words were curt, cutting the conversation short. The warm, fluttery feelings were driving her up the wall, and she didn't like feeling out of control.

Especially before her event. Even more so since the fluttery feelings were for a guy she swore never to trust.

"Ty, thanks for your concern," she added, as she eased the halter down Red's nose and slipped the bit into her horse's mouth. "I'm good. Your conscience can be eased."

He scowled at her.

Bingo. That was exactly why he was here.

"I'm not easing my conscience," he said, his voice gravelly.

"I don't have time for it either way. I need to focus." She had a race ahead of her, and the last thing she wanted was Ty Hartman and that sexy gaze of his bleeding into her thoughts when her focus should be on winning.

"Fine." Ty reached into his pocket and pulled out a small white card. "Here."

He took her hand and shoved the card into it, crumpling the edges against her palm, as the calluses on his fingers brushed against the sensitive skin of her fingertips.

Her fingers flexed inward toward his own, trapping the card against her palm.

"Just in case you need my number." He jerked his chin at her hands.

"I don't—" She was cut off by the announcer.

"AND UP NEXT—BARREL RACING." The words rang clear across the rodeo grounds. "We'll take a short break as we set up the arena."

"Oh shoot!" Ella spun away from Ty. "I've got to go."

She crammed the card in her back pocket without looking at it.

Red was giving her a horsey look of "about time" and stamped her hoof as the puppy continued to yap.

Ella's heart slammed against her ribs, the feeling amplified by each sharp puppy bark. Slipping her foot into the stirrup, she tried to swing up, but Red danced sideways.

"Red," Ella said, the word squeaking out of her throat, tightened with nerves. She pushed up again, but Red wasn't having it, and she couldn't get the momentum to swing into the saddle.

"Here." Ty's voice was a deep grumble, and he grabbed the reins to hold Red in place, his body close enough that she could smell the scent of pine and leather as she mounted the horse.

"Thanks," she muttered, barely able to look at him. The small white card felt like it was burning in her back pocket.

She nudged Red forward and was immediately stopped by a blond woman on a big buckskin horse passing by. Ella tried not to roll her eyes as Lindsey Whitmore looked her up and down, the other woman's lip lifted in a look of disdain.

Lindsey had once been her friend in high school when Ella started seeing moderate success at barrels. Ella had been so enamored with the fact that the prettiest and richest girl in school wanted to be friends with her, that she hadn't even bothered to ask why Lindsey was suddenly friendly with her. It was the first time Ella had felt truly accepted by her peers, and that year had been one of the best times of her life.

Then she started beating Lindsey at barrels.

Lindsey claimed she didn't care, but it was impossible to ignore the fact her friend was growing distant and her remarks became more cutting. Ella finally couldn't ignore it any longer when she overheard Lindsey plotting with her friends to have one of the most popular boys in school ask Ella to prom—only to ditch her the night of the event.

And, of course, she had told Lindsey the week before about her crush on Ty. Leave it to Lindsey to seek revenge once Ella become legitimate rodeo competition.

"Back on the ugliest horse on this planet, huh?" Lindsey quirked an eyebrow at her before riding away. Ella opened her mouth to comment but swallowed the words back. Lindsey wasn't worth it, and she still needed to warm up.

Long-trotting over to the warm-up arena, Ella took Red through a few quick rounds until Red's focus was entirely on her and the only thing on her mind was the race ahead of her.

"Ella Sanders, on deck," the announcer called.

Her heart lurched, but this time, rather than feeling queasy, she clenched her hands firmly around the reins.

She needed this win.

Urging Red forward, they headed to the arena, arriving just as the cowgirl ahead of her finished her run.

"Aaaaand uuup is Ella James Sanders," the announcer

drawled. "Keep an eye on this home-grown cowgirl and her horse Red. Just because Red isn't the prettiest mare to look at doesn't mean this horse doesn't know her barrels. This is Ella's first year on the pro-rodeo circuit, and this feisty cowgirl is blasting through the ranks."

The crowd's roar echoed in her ears as Red pranced into place. This was their shared love. What bonded them as a pair. Red lived for the barrels.

Red breaths came in short, heavy bursts as the horse's muscles bunched under the saddle. For a split second, time held still, the nerves disappeared, and then they were off like a shot. Red flew into the arena full speed as her hooves pounded into the sand. Ella glared down the first barrel and seated herself tight into the saddle as they set up their pocket and whipped around the first of three.

The wind roared in her ears, blocking out any sound. Their entire focus, every breath, every second was centered on the barrel in front of them.

Ella switched her hands on the rein and saddle cantle as they approached the second barrel. Red pivoted around it, her muscles bunching in powerful bursts, before they launched toward the third and final barrel.

The third barrel was always Red's most challenging, as they frequently cut the pocket a bit too close.

They approached the barrel at breakneck speed, Red slowing down just enough to whirl around it. Ella could feel the edge of metal brush against her knee, but she didn't look back as they raced toward the finish line. Red's strides ate up ground so fast Ella wondered if her horse's hooves even touched the sand.

There was a split second of silence as she and her horse circled to a stop. Both of them were panting and sweat was worked up on Red's coat. Blood thrummed in Ella's ears as she strained to hear her time.

"Whoop!" she yelled as the announcer called out a personal best.

"And that, ladies and gents, will place Ella at the top of the list. Boy, howdy, that was a helluva run, cowgirl! Thanks, Ella," the announcer called. Ella smiled and waved at the crowd before exiting the arena.

Nothing, absolutely nothing, was going to bring her down for the rest of the day. Even if Lindsey won the competition, she and Red had marked a personal best.

Red snorted, tossing her head as she pranced back to the trailer, too worked up to slow to a walk.

There were only three more cowgirls left, but at this point, it was out of her control. Right now, she needed to cool Red down, untack, unwind, and then head home. They had a long drive ahead of them.

People waved and called out "nice run" as she worked her way back to the trailer; Red fighting against the restraint of the reins and her tiedown. Thankfully, the puppy was nowhere in sight.

"Easy, girl," Ella said, pulling gently on the reins. "I'm just going to grab some water, and then we can cool down."

Red halted but energy radiated from every inch of the horse's muscular body. Gripping the reins and Red's mane in one hand, Ella swung her leg up and over. Out of the corner of her eye, she spotted the little, blue-speckled puppy sprinting out from behind the truck, boisterously yapping its head off.

And at the exact moment, some asshole honked their horn.

Red lost it.

Caught off guard by the sudden blare, Red reacted the way any high-strung horse would react—she spooked. The horse dropped down so suddenly Ella could feel air under her before she too dropped. One foot was still caught in the stirrup, trapping her in place. Ella clung to the horn, digging her fingernails painfully into the leather as Red bolted sideways, desperate to escape from whatever horse monster the truck and puppy turned out to be. Ella's body jerked from Red's sudden movement, twisting her body, but her foot caught in the stirrup didn't move. A sharp pain tore from her knee, up her back and to her brain.

A cry ripped from her throat as she struggled to free her foot while clinging to the tiny saddle horn.

Finally, the stirrup popped off. The reins slid through her fingers, and she collapsed to the ground just in time to see Red, her usually trustworthy steed, take off toward the warm-up arena at a mad gallop.

There was the third bad event for the day.

CHAPTER TWO

"SOMEONE GET THE EMT," a man shouted.

Ella lay in shock, her back flat against the ground. Pain reverberated through her body as she tried to wrap her mind around what just happened.

Tightening her jaw, she tried to scramble to her feet, but her knee wasn't responding like it should. Heat and pain tore through her as she tried to stand.

The silky clay dirt clung to her hands and pale jeans. The man who demanded the EMT slipped his hands under her arms and helped her to her feet. She shifted her weight onto both legs and then collapsed against the man's chest as blinding pain screamed from her knee.

"I've got ya," the guy muttered, catching her before she dropped back into the dirt. Tucking his shoulder under her arm, he helped her to the edge of the trailer just as two men with black vests identifying themselves as medical professionals hustled over.

The EMTs made quick work of assessing the situation, asking questions about what happened as they checked her for injures.

Minutes later, Ty showed up, leading her now-docile horse behind him, the mare's head hanging low.

Of course Ty found her horse.

She couldn't quite make eye contact with him as he unbridled her mare and slipped her halter back on. Running her eyes over her horse, she was relieved to see that the mare didn't appear to be impacted by the accident.

"You may have torn a ligament in your knee," the EMT said gently. "It's swelling significantly. I'd recommend you go to the hospital as soon as possible for an MRI."

She stared back at the EMT. "I'm sorry, what?"

"You need an MRI," he repeated patiently. "Do you have someone who can drive you to the hospital?"

She opened her mouth. Closed it. Swallowed. Her tongue was incredibly dry and too large for her mouth. Jordan had already left, and there was no one else she trusted to take her to the hospital.

On top of that, she couldn't afford an MRI. Not now. Not when she was just at the point of earning enough for a down payment for her dream ranch.

Her face felt hot and swollen, and if she didn't do something soon, she'd probably cry.

She pressed the backs of her hands against her eyes.

"Do you have anyone who can take you to the hospital?" the EMT repeated. "We can take you in an ambulance."

There was no way she was getting into an ambulance and racking up that medical bill.

She shook her head.

"My friend already left to head home." To her horror, her voice caught on the last word.

"I can drive her."

Her breath caught. She didn't need to look up to know it was Ty who spoke.

"You know her?" the man in the black vest asked.

"We're both from Garnet Valley." Ty continued untacking Red, stashing the saddle and the bridle in her tack room and moving through the motions as though it were his own trailer. "I can take her to the hospital and drive her home."

Forget the ambulance, there was no way on this living earth she was going to spend multiple hours with Ty on a drive back to Garnet Valley. Much less have him wait for her in the hospital.

"I'm fine, guys. I just need a minute to recover." Except that her knee looked like a water balloon ready to burst.

Though every instinct in her body told her not to, she shifted her weight into her leg and tried to stand. One sharp, stabbing second later, she collapsed back on the edge of the trailer.

Shit.

She looked around the area for anyone else she knew. Literally anyone who wasn't Ty Hartman.

No one showed up. She glanced at Ty, who was brushing her horse's damp coat in quick circles with a curry comb.

"I can drive myself," she said reluctantly.

Her pulsing knee disagreed. As did the look on the EMT's face.

Ty paused his brushing. "I don't think that's wise. What if the hospital puts you on pain meds? You can't drive a truck and trailer in that condition."

"I'll wait until I'm home to take the pain meds," she

huffed. If only her knee would cooperate.

"I'll drive you," he repeated firmly, as though his mind was made up, and she was supposed to just follow his lead.

"What about your truck? And Red?" She was now scrambling for excuses.

"I came here with my brother. We can take my rig. I'll ask Colton if he can drive your truck and Red home." Ty's voice was gruff.

"No, Red—"

"Will be fine," Ty insisted. "Colton is damn good with horses, and you know it."

The complaint died on her lips. Colton was good with horses. Or at least he had been before he left Garnet Valley over a decade ago. She looked around, searching for a reason to insist on driving herself, when she noticed the small crowd formed around them.

"It's Ella Sanders," someone whispered.

"Shame," someone else said softly. "Is she okay? I'd hate to see her out for the rest of the year."

And that's when it hit her. If she didn't act now, this could impact the rest of her season and her chances of going to the NFR. If she didn't have her rodeo earnings to save, her dream of owning a ranch, training horses, and proving she was a winner was at risk. There was no way she could live off her waitressing income alone and continue saving for her down payment.

She had to put aside her pride.

Even if that meant being stuck with Ty Hartman, the guy who she didn't trust, yet for some crazy reason, couldn't keep her eyes off of.

"Fine. I'll go," she relented.

Ty gave a breath of relief.

"Give me five minutes to make a few calls and get my truck over here." Ty pulled his cell phone out of his back pocket.

Minutes later, Ty's expensive blue truck appeared with Colton Hartman behind the wheel and his girlfriend Gus Jones in the passenger seat.

She tried to return Gus's friendly smile but had a feeling that the attempt fell flat.

"Don't worry about Red," Colton assured her. "Do you want me to keep her at our place or drop her at yours?"

Her mind raced as she tried to figure out the best approach for her horse.

"Keep her at ours. I can drop Red off tomorrow," Ty said gruffly. He pulled his brother aside. Whatever he was saying, it was too low for Ella to catch. Ty jerked his head toward her horse, and Colton nodded, running his hand over his jaw.

She closed her eyes and tried to ignore the fact that Ty had guaranteed she would see him tomorrow.

"And cool her down, please," Ella groaned as Ty broke away from his brother and positioned his body next to her.

"I'm going to help you up." Ty leaned down to wrap an arm around her ribs and slowly straightened, giving her time to scramble to her feet.

"You got it?" the EMTs asked Ty.

"I've got it." He tucked his arm under her shoulders, pressing the full length of his body against hers, supporting her weight as she limped to Ty's truck. "You doing okay, cowgirl?"

The position of his body had his voice right next to her ear. His breath tickled the sensitive shell, and something about the soothing way he asked, made her lips quiver.

She pressed her lips together, biting down on them to suppress any chance of crying.

The last thing she wanted was for Ty to see her at her weakest. She didn't want to be vulnerable with Ty. Not now. Not ever.

He shifted his strong arms around her waist as he helped her into the cab of his truck.

Once inside, she settled into the leather seats. Dropping her head against the headrest, she closed her eyes, suddenly exhausted.

The inside of the truck smelled like Ty—leather, soap, and some sort of pine.

"Focus," she muttered to herself as Ty shut her door and went around to the other side.

The muscles around her knee screamed as she twisted to pull the seat belt over her shoulder.

Ty opened the door and climbed in behind the wheel. Ella froze, belt in her hand.

The mere presence of the man somehow made the cab of his truck shrink to the size of a sugar cube.

"Everything okay?" Ty's eyes were piercing, as though he were trying to read her mind.

"Dandy, Ty. My knee feels like it's been ripped in half, my horse is going home with someone else, and I'm worried about my season. Everything is just peachy." She yanked on the seat belt, but it caught, jerking to a stop. She tugged again, but the emergency latch refused to let go.

"Easy on the sarcasm, cowgirl." Ty leaned over the center console, closer to her.

Her heart hammered in her chest, threatening to burst free. This was too much. She didn't want a ride from Ty. She didn't want Red to go home with Colton. She wanted to find out if she won, take her pot, and add it to the growing pile of savings she had. She didn't want to worry if this was her last rodeo of the season. Or ever.

Opening her mouth, she pulled in a shaky breath. There was no way she was going to cry.

"Hey, hey, cowgirl. It's okay." Ty's voice was soothing, like he was calming a spooked horse. He reached over, his shoulder brushing against hers as he peeled her fingers from around the seat belt, the rough calluses of his hands brushing against hers.

This close, she could see the hint of five-o'clock shadow along the sharp line of his jaw.

His scent seemed to envelop her, and for a second, she almost forgot how much pain she was in.

He smelled so good.

Some crazy part of her wanted to press her face against his shoulder, breath him in, and hear him tell her it was going to be okay over and over again.

The logical side of her knew not to show weakness. Ty wouldn't want to deal with her tears, and she didn't want to share them.

Slowly, Ty fed the seat belt back up, the action forcing his body even closer. So close she found herself staring at his firm, well-cut lips.

Heat bloomed through her, warming her to her core.

"Did I place?" she asked, the only words that seemed willing to come out.

"I'll call when we get you to the hospital."

Her lips parted as he pulled the seat belt out and over her body, buckling it into place at her hips.

Ty looked up, his hands still at the buckle. The air between them tightened, as though he was silently bidding her closer.

"On to the hospital," Ty said, his voice gruff.

She nodded, unable to speak, her knee throbbing.

Breaking eye contact, Ty pulled the truck into gear and slowly eased away from the crowd and out of the rodeo grounds.

Ella smiled at the people who waved as she left. After all, even in pain, a cowgirl had to be tough.

Would these people even care about her if she were no longer a top contender?

Hopefully, she'd never have to find out.

"I owe you for this," she said as Ty maneuvered the rig toward the hospital. Her father would kill her if he found out she was in debt to a Hartman. Heck, she wasn't thrilled about it herself. "I hope I don't get you in trouble with the rodeo board."

"No worries," Ty said. "I just want to make sure you're okay."

And being Ty, she had no doubt he would be able to smooth everything over. Everything always went his way.

"I'll figure out a way to pay you back," she insisted, adjusting her seat so that she could straighten her leg a bit more.

"Hmm," Ty said. "How about I keep that in the back of my mind?"

"Sounds good," she muttered.

"You could share with me what about me you don't like," he offered.

She looked at him from the corner of her eyes. How did he not know her issues with him?

"Maybe this is how I am around people," she countered. It was much easier to fend off the comment than deal with it right now.

"No," Ty insisted. "I've seen you around other people. This is how you treat me."

"Maybe you're just special." She closed her eyes and turned her head toward the window, pressing her forehead against the cool glass.

Ty must have taken the hint because he didn't press further. Exhausted, wiped, and emotionally drained, she didn't have the energy to fight him. Closing her eyes, she tried to focus on something besides the pain radiating through her leg.

Unfortunately, the only thing that kept coming to mind was the impact to her career.

She'd been riding high all season. She just hadn't expected to come crashing down so hard so fast.

TY PACED THE length of the waiting room, ignoring the glares of the four people sitting in the plastic chairs against the walls. There was no way he could sit until he saw Ella again.

The second he'd seen Red weaving through the line of horse trailers, head held high, saddle skewed on her back, Ty had known something was wrong. As much as he swore that he was going to avoid Ella after checking on her this afternoon, he couldn't let her horse run wild and not follow up with her.

Seeing Ella pale and crumpled on the edge of the horse trailer had been a shock. As a vet, he hated seeing animals injured. Turned out he hated seeing Ella injured just as much. She had always seemed so resilient, so strong for as long as he had known her. Seeing her injured made him realize just how vulnerable she was.

There was no way he could have left her there at the fairgrounds on her own and hurting. Even if it led to a long, awkward drive home.

He ran his hand over his face. Worse, he thought he had caught a slight limp in Red as he had led the horse back to the trailer. Not enough that he was concerned, but that tiny, almost impossible to perceive hitch in her step worried him. Good thing the mare was staying on the Rocking H so he could check on her in the morning.

Giving up on the pacing, he dropped down into a plastic chair. The last time he was in a hospital was after his dad's auto accident, and his dad never walked out.

He let out a breath, trying to suppress the memory. During the hours he had spent there, he had pulled his phone out a zillion times to call his mom and to call Colton, and he couldn't bring himself to do it. He hadn't been ready to admit his dad was gone. It had taken him forty-five minutes to work up the courage to call Colton.

The soft sound of the double doors opening broke the silence and interrupted his thoughts.

"Ty?"

At the sound of Ella's voice, he leapt to his feet. He took one look at her, and his stomach dropped.

A nurse wheeled her into the waiting room. A large black brace was wrapped around her knee, crutches lay on her lap, and her eyes were too wide for her pale face. Her chin stuck stubbornly out, like she was trying to be tough even though she also looked ready to crumble. It took everything he had to not wrap his arms around her and tell her it would be okay.

He wanted to. More than anything.

Without thinking, he took her hand and squeezed. Ella had to be in shock because her fingers curled into his, and his heart leapt against his ribs.

"You look terrible," he said, opting for honesty.

Her lips were so pale, they looked white. Her dark hair was stark against her chalky skin.

She pulled her fingers away. "I'm filled to the brim with pain meds, I'm exhausted, and my knee ligament, or something like that, is torn. Of course I look terrible, you jerk," she said, her words slightly slurred with the effects of the pain meds.

Alright maybe now wasn't the time for honesty, but no one ever accused him of being smooth. This was why he was much better with animals than people. Animals never took offense to honesty.

"Will you need surgery?" he asked.

She shook her head. "Doctor doesn't think so. He recommends my doctor reassess once the swelling goes down."

He followed Ella and the nurse out of the hospital, pulling his jacket around him as they stepped out into the cool night air.

"Will it put you in a better mood to hear you won your event?" he tried again.

"It will if we can stop to buy a milkshake on our way home," she grumbled. "I left my sandwich in my truck."

Once outside the hospital entrance, he helped her up from the wheelchair.

"I've got it." Her voice was small and uneven as she pushed away his hands.

He hated that defeat in her voice. The Ella he knew was strong and invincible. This timid one, the hurt one, roused his protective instincts. Only he knew she didn't want his help.

He followed as she crutched her way to his truck parked two spots down. He moved ahead to open the door and help her in.

The night sky overhead revealed an oversized moon and billions of stars. The fall air had cooled to the point that the evening's breeze was sharp at the open neck of his jacket. He looked at Ella's thin plaid shirt.

"Do you need a coat?" he offered.

She shook her head, and he helped her into the truck.

A few minutes later, the heater was cranked on, Ella's crutches were in the backseat, and he found a drive-thru to pick up a couple burgers and her requested milkshake. Ella insisted on paying.

Then they were on the road. There were at least a couple hours before they were back in Garnet Valley.

Except for the occasional wash of headlights from an oncoming truck, the late night made it seem like they were the only two people on the rural highway. The truck was silent, the sound of tires on the road the only noise for the first ten minutes until he turned on a country station.

His body seemed to be attuned to Ella, who did not seem remotely comfortable. She kept shifting, the fabric of her clothes rubbing against the seat. Her knee was rigid in the brace, and she crossed and uncrossed her arms. Finally, she slumped against the window, pressing her forehead against the glass.

"I'm sorry this happened," he said.

"Me too."

The subtle scent of her shampoo—coconut—filled the small space, and the memory of her body pressed along the side of his as he helped her to his truck flashed into his mind. They'd been in the middle of the busy fairgrounds, but the feel of her curves molded against him had imprinted on his body and burned in his brain.

He pressed the back of his head against his headrest, trying to figure out what to say when he heard soft sniffles coming from her side of the cab.

Damn it. He didn't want her to cry.

"Ella…" He gentled his voice to the one he used with scared animals.

"It's nothing." Her voice was watery, and he could hear her body shift to twist farther away from him, closing him off.

"Let me know if there's anything I can do," he said, wondering why he was even bothering.

"I'm fine."

Brush-off complete. It had to be her tears that made him keep trying. Or just straight insanity. "I could have Colton help with Red while you're out."

"No," she said flatly. It was the same brook-no-arguments tone she always used on him.

"Why not?" he countered, unable to stop himself from pressing her.

"Because I can't afford to have Colton workout Red, and, besides that, I think my family has had enough bad experiences dealing with the Hartmans."

Ty ran his hand down his face. It didn't surprise him that her father Jared was still pissed about that.

"Look, your father owed us the money. It wasn't my fault that your dad had to sell the horses." The year Beau had called in the debt had been a lean year, and it wasn't just the Sanders. Beau had to call in all the loans to help the ranch survive.

"You took my rodeo horse and the only workhorse my dad had." Her words were sharp. She was clearly still upset about the situation. "We nearly lost everything because my dad didn't have a horse to ride when ranches needed help. It was a big loss of income for us."

And Ella had to borrow a horse to continue high school rodeo.

"Ella—"

"I don't want to hear your excuses," she muttered, her face still directed at the window.

Fine. "What about all your earnings?"

Silence. And not that soft, quiet, crying silence. It was a

tense, furious, he-had-crossed-a-line silence.

"Not everyone just gets to dump their rodeo winnings into the next horse or trailer or trainer or whatever." Her voice was soft, but the irritation carried. "Some of us are still paying off student loan debts and trying to save for a ranch."

He hadn't known that. Then again, why would he? It wasn't like they talked.

Out of the corner of his eye, he saw Ella shift her head against the window, trying to get comfortable.

He chewed his lip.

"Can we talk later?" Ella mumbled. Her voice soft and distant. "I need to sleep."

"Go ahead," he said, keeping his gaze on the road ahead.

The rest of the trip was silent. As they neared her place, Ty looked over at her sleeping form, her arms wrapped around herself, and her face turned away from him. She looked soft. Vulnerable.

He scrubbed his hand over his jaw. It was just past midnight, and he was ready to be in bed. "Ella, wake up. We're almost there."

She didn't stir.

His fingers itched to touch her. Just to see if that spark when she was near was real.

He kept his hand firmly on the steering wheel.

"Ella."

"Hmm?" She shifted as he turned onto her street and parked in front of her tiny home. The same place she grew up. She kept the place when her parents moved to Oregon.

"We're here."

This area of town looked different at night. It was hard to tell just how worn the little trailers and porches were.

"How do you feel?" he asked.

"Groggy. And hurting. I just need some decent sleep, and some time to mope," she said with that familiar bluntness that made him smile. "Do you know if Colton and Red made it back okay?"

"Red is fine. Colton got home an hour ago. That mare is in the best hands possible."

"I know," Ella said. "Can you bring her over first thing tomorrow? I want my own eyes on her."

He opened his mouth to voice his concern with Red but stopped himself. Ella had enough on her plate tonight, and Red may walk it off by tomorrow morning. It wasn't even a limp at the fairgrounds. Just a tiny hitch in her step. He may have even imagined it during the stress of the situation. However, he did have Colton wrap her legs before taking her home. Better safe than sorry.

He eased out of the truck. The night air in Garnet Valley was cooler than in Dillon, and he wanted to get her inside as quickly as possible.

Ella pushed the passenger side door open, but she was struggling to get out. He eased her down, her waist warm against his hands.

There was a small pen to one side of her trailer with a tiny stack of hay. A lone horse nickered softly, and Ella veered toward the haystack.

"I've got it," Ty said, reaching for the flakes of hay before she could argue. It must have been pure exhaustion, or she was in that much pain, because she stayed silent as he tossed the food into a tire feeder.

The wind pushed her hair across her face, as they continued to the front of her place.

"You didn't need to walk me to the door." Ella crutched up the three crooked steps before struggling to pull the keys out of her pocket. He let her curse silently to herself, knowing that unless she asked for help, he should let her sort herself out. Finally, she freed the ring from her pocket and unlocked the front door. The dead bolt clicked back, but she didn't move to open it.

"It'll be eight to ten weeks until I'm back in the saddle." She spoke to the door, keeping her back to him.

"I know you'll be back on a horse as soon as you are able," he said, trying to find some way to comfort her.

She didn't answer. The only sound were the crickets in the back fields.

"I'm sure you're tired. Do you need any help before I leave?" he offered.

"I'm good." Her voice was heavy with exhaustion.

"You'll call if you need anything?" He didn't mean to ask, but he couldn't stop himself.

"Let me pay you for gas." She pulled her wallet out of her back pocket and took the remaining bills from it. "I hope twenty is enough."

He pushed her hand away. "No worries."

"Seriously." She shoved the cash in his hand before turning away and opening the front door.

"You can let me help you without paying me back."

"No. I don't want to owe you anything, Ty Hartman. I don't want to be obligated to you, or anyone, in any way."

"That's not what's going on," he started to say but she was already inside, awkwardly maneuvering on her crutches to close the door.

"I'm only trying to help." The familiar warmth he got whenever he was around her stirred through him.

Ella closed the door until all he could see was her face, pinched tight and exhausted. She bit her lip and didn't quite look at him.

"Ty?" Her voice was soft and laced with fatigue.

"Yes?"

"Thank you for everything, but after you drop Red off tomorrow, I won't need anything else."

In other words, she was rejecting any help before he could even offer.

As he headed back to his truck, he told himself it was okay. Ella was setting boundaries, and he'd respect that.

But the fact that she was hurting and on her own bothered him.

Chapter Three

B Y THE TIME Ty got home, the only thing awake were the crickets. Ella's truck and trailer were parked behind the barn, and everyone was fast asleep.

It wasn't until the next morning that Ty saw either of his brothers.

"How's Ella?" Colton asked as Ty wandered into the kitchen wearing a pair of faded jeans and a white undershirt. His brother was in worn Wranglers and gray boot socks, the sleeves of his blue plaid button-up rolled up to his elbows. His brother looked like he never lived a day outside Montana. Hard to believe that only a few months ago it had taken everything Ty had to convince Colton to stick around for the year.

Now Colton was dating Gus, happily in love, and appeared to have zero intentions of leaving any time soon.

Ty rubbed his growling stomach as he inhaled the scent of fried eggs and bacon. Outside of breakfast, Colton couldn't cook a meal to save his life, but he certainly had breakfast down.

"Smells good," Ty commented, pouring himself a cup of coffee and moving to the kitchen island. "She's not doing so hot. Tore some ligament in her knee and looks like she is out for the rest of the season. She's got eight weeks or so until she heals." He dropped down onto a stool at the kitchen island. "I'll check on her when I drop Red off."

Colton sucked in a breath and his brows drew together. "About that. Have you looked at that mare yet?"

That didn't sound good. Ty straightened and glanced out the kitchen bay window to see the sorrel mare in a pen by the barn. "It was darker than hell when I got home, and I just woke up. Why?"

Colton sighed. "I got her home last night, and she was limping. It was too dark to tell, but I looked at her this morning, and she's clearly injured."

"Shit." Coffee sloshed over the edge of the cup as he banged it against the counter and headed to the mudroom for his boots. Ella was going to kill him. "Did you wrap her legs before traveling last night?"

"Of course I did," Colton said as Ty yanked on his boots. "Do you want me to head out with you?"

"Not right now. If I need help, I'll let you know." He was used to doing things on his own anyway.

He hustled out the front door, his vet instinct on high alert.

The fall day was going to be a hot one, that was for sure. The air was dry, making each breath feel like he had dust rattling in his lungs as he headed down the wooden porch, pausing to grab Red's black halter that Colton had hung on the end hook.

The morning sun glinted off rich green stalks of alfalfa growing in the nearby field, and the glare hit him right in the eyes. He blocked the light with his hand, wishing he had grabbed a hat.

His brother had put the horse in one of the empty pens next to the barn. It was a smaller pen, so the mare couldn't move around too much, which was ideal for an injured animal.

Even before he got close, he could tell something was off. The horse was holding her body stiffly as she moved slowly around the enclosure. Sure enough, the mare was favoring her left front leg.

Ella was going to be furious. No doubt this happened yesterday at the rodeo. Sometimes it took a few hours for the injury to show itself when it was a tendon, and it looked like this was the case with Red. It was possible that the trailer ride exacerbated the injury, but Colton had done what he could by wrapping her legs.

How he was going to explain this to Ella, he didn't know. She had enough on her plate with her own injury, and now he had to add her horse's injury on top of that.

He made a quick detour to the grain shed to grab a pail of oats. Then, before he headed to Red's pen, he forced himself to stop and take a deep breath, to calm the twist of panic in his gut. Horses were very intuitive and could sense moods and emotions. He wanted to be as calm as possible with a horse that was unfamiliar with him. As he had learned a long time ago, you had to be careful around animals whose instinct was to react first and think later. Especially when the animal was injured. That made them even more vulnerable to predators.

Red's wide nostrils quivered as he approached, and he could make out the edge of white around her eyes.

The leggy, muscular mare backed up until her butt pressed against the back panel of fence. He shook the oats in the pail, letting the horse know that there was a tasty snack waiting for her.

Stretching out her neck, the mare's mouth started to soften. Calmly, he entered the enclosure and quietly approached her, shaking the oats until Red's nose was in the pail. Dropping the bucket to the ground, he looped the halter over Red's nose and behind her ears.

It only took a short assessment to confirm that things didn't look good.

"What's the prognosis?" Colton asked as Ty came through the front door.

He shook his head and ran his hand over his hair. "Not good. I'd need to do an ultrasound, but it looks like a sprain right around her cannon bone. It's a nasty place for an injury and can take some time to heal. I'm going to have to leave her here for now. The trip to town is too rough and could cause further injury. I'd rather be safe than sorry."

"You going to help her out?" Colton pulled a warmed tortilla from the oven and started wrapping eggs, bacon, potatoes, and cheese into burritos. On any other day, Ty would be pacing for the burritos to finish. Today his mind was too busy to care.

"Hmm." Ty grabbed the lukewarm mug of coffee he left on the counter. He'd like to help. Only... "I think she would rather throw herself off a bridge than accept my help."

His brother chuckled. "I've always liked her."

Ty rubbed at his ribs. "And she's never liked me."

And judging from what little she said during the ride home, her old rodeo horse was one of the reasons why.

Feeling a buzz in his pocket, Ty pulled out his phone.

Mom. The last person he wanted to deal with.

Shaking his head, he silenced the call, and stuck the device back in his pocket.

Since his father passed away, his mom had been trying to reach out to him. He saw her at the funeral, which was the first time he'd seen her in Montana since she had left for Idaho almost a decade ago, and ever since, she'd been trying to contact him.

He wasn't ready to open himself back up to her again. There was enough on his plate without adding his mom to the pile.

He leaned against the kitchen table and stared out at the field from the big bay window. Red had pushed the flake of hay he had tossed into her feeder into a fluffy mess of stalks and leaves. Her weight was firmly planted on three legs with the front leg cocked.

If he was to go back to ignoring Ella, working with her injured horse wasn't ideal, but he couldn't ignore an injured animal. That wasn't his way.

However... An interesting thought began to form in the back of his mind.

"I'll talk with her about it this morning when I head over. What are you up to this morning after chores?"

"Gus and I are heading to Bozeman to pick up supplies." Colton's girlfriend, Gus, was contracted to repair the ranch buildings with Colton helping out when he had the time. They were in a big crunch to wrap up as much of the exterior work as possible before the winter weather came in.

Some small part of him wished that they wouldn't work so hard to stay on track. The longer it took to repair the ranch, the more time he had to save up money to buy one of his brothers' shares of the ranch.

Now that Colton was dating Gus, it was clear one brother wasn't going to leave Montana any time soon; however, he still wasn't sure what Jace's plan was, and his concern was that the eldest Hartman would want to sell.

If he had more time, he could try to convince Jace to stay. Otherwise, all his savings would go to the ranch, and his plans to expand his vet practice to the ranch would be on hold for years.

"Morning." Jace wandered into the kitchen, wearing worn Levi's that Ty had lent him months ago and a gray tee. "Can we get started on chores early? I'm heading to the airport in an hour to pick up Hailey."

Jace's wife was still flying between their homes in Houston and Montana, which made Ty even more certain that Jace had zero interest in sticking around after their year probation was up.

"Only seven more months of this," Jace muttered as he poured himself a cup of coffee and sat down next to Ty.

Jutting out his jaw, Ty folded his arms and continued to study Red from the window. The conversation with Roy and Josh from the Dillon rodeo floated to the front of his mind.

Maybe Red's injury was a good opportunity for him. Not that he wanted a horse to get injured, but maybe this was his chance to test out the pressure point therapy he'd been dying to try. If word got around the rodeo circuit that he was the vet responsible for rehabilitating the well-known barrel horse, it could bring him more business. That would let him save up more to buy out Jace and at the same time grow his client list to let him expand his practice at a faster rate.

And if Jace stuck around, he'd have more cash to throw into his new vet operation. The last string to tie was having his brothers okay his plan since they had equal ownership of the ranch, but he couldn't imagine that being a hard sell.

It was a win-win for him.

He just needed to convince Red's owner that this was the best for the horse. Which it was.

ELLA WOKE UP to her body aching, her knee screaming in pain, and a headache that wouldn't quit.

Sun filtered through the open windows, glaring against her closed eyelids. She'd been in too much pain to even think about drawing the curtains last night.

Blocking the bright light with her hand, she gingerly eased to the edge of the bed and grabbed her phone.

Shoot. She had three missed calls from Jordan, followed by two text messages, and another text from Ty twenty minutes ago saying that he was heading to her place.

Which meant he would be here any minute. She was still in her pajamas.

And she hadn't fed her animals yet.

Careful to not jar her leg, she strapped on the cumbersome brace. Shoving the crutches under her sore arms, she pushed to her feet and headed to the bathroom.

One glance in the bathroom mirror stopped her cold. Long messy locks had escaped the bun she had thrown her hair into before bed. Dark circles ringed her eyes. And her usual golden skin looked pale, creating a stark contrast with her dark hair.

She looked like a disaster zone without the warning sign.

Grabbing her toothbrush, she quickly brushed her teeth and was just about to pull her hair free of the messy bun when the sound of tires on gravel carried through her open window followed by the alert bark of her dog.

Her fingers froze on her hair tie.

That had to be Ty.

Her stomach gave her a weird fluttery feeling as she pushed her fingers into her hair. She looked like hell, and the worn pajama shorts and black tank weren't helping.

She itched to grab her tinted moisturizer and mascara and attempt to make herself look partway presentable. The last thing she wanted was for Ty to see her in this state.

The knock at the door echoed through the small trailer. Ella dropped her hands to the sink and gripped the edge.

"One minute," she called, wondering what the hell to fix first—her hair or her clothes.

Changing would take too long, especially with the brace.

Pulling her hair out of its bun, she shook out her tresses. Normally her hair would fall into soft waves after being tied up, but today was the day it decided to go off course. Her ends stuck out at awkward angles, stubbornly refusing to frame her face at anything other than a ninety-degree bend.

Another knock.

Pressing her hand against her forehead, she looked wildly around. She caught her reflection again in the mirror, her eyes wide.

You know what? Screw it. It didn't matter what Ty thought. She learned her lesson before with an attractive cowboy. Once was enough.

On that note, she gripped her crutches firmly and headed to the front door, her head pounding with each swing of her body.

The September air felt cool on her legs as she pulled open the flimsy front door and pushed the screen door away, nearly smacking Ty in the face with it.

"Hey there," Ty said, catching the door easily before it collided with him. Moving onto the porch, she closed her front door behind her.

There was no way she was going to let a cowboy who had a whole homestead to his name see the inside of her tiny trailer. It wasn't that she was ashamed—this was the place she grew up. It had enough land to keep her horses, neighbors she loved, and the rent was cheap so she could save as much as possible. It was that people judged where she came from, and there was no way she was going to give them more ammo.

"Morning," she muttered, tucking her wayward hair behind her ear and wondering what angle it was at now.

"I would ask how you slept, but I think I know the answer." His voice held a hint of gravel that sent another dart of warmth through her as his eyes took in her face.

And to think she once had a crush on this charmer.

She narrowed her eyes. "If you're judging my hair, I woke

up like this, thank you very much," she said drily. "Not everyone can crawl out of bed and look flawless."

Especially after tearing some ligaments in her knee. The tears were thankfully in a good location and didn't appear to be impacting the stability of her knee. However, that didn't mean it didn't feel like someone was stabbing a white-hot knife into the joint.

"I don't think you look bad at all."

She rolled her eyes. A retort was sharp and ready on her tongue, but before she could spit it out, his blue gaze raked her from head to toe, careful, assessing. Warming. And the words evaporated on her lips.

His jaw tightened as he took in the hemline of her shorts and the top of the brace. Her body seemed to light up the entire trail his gaze blazed down and then back up. Then without a word, Ty handed her a foil baking pan.

"What's this?" She eyed it suspiciously.

Ty shrugged. "It was on your porch when I arrived. Someone probably heard about your accident and dropped it off."

"Weird." There was no way this was from Ms. Minna. While she always made pies or cakes, she wouldn't just drop it off on her porch. And Mrs. Thompson and her husband were currently out of town visiting family.

He pressed his lips together. "Why would that be weird?"

Of course Ty wouldn't think it was strange. The whole community pulled together after his father's funeral, and probably at every low point in his life.

Meanwhile, this was the first meal she had ever received that wasn't from one of her two neighbors.

And there was no name or note on the dish. That seemed suspicious. She opened her mouth to say so when something— or rather lack of something—caught her eye.

Wait a minute.

Shoving the baking dish back into Ty's hands, she crutched to the edge of the porch.

Parked right in the middle of her driveway was Ty's dark blue truck. And nothing else.

"Where's my truck?" she demanded. She looked up and down the street to make sure she hadn't missed it. "And trailer?" More importantly. "Where is my horse?"

Her voice had an edge she couldn't hide.

If Ty hadn't brought her horse that could only mean—

Her heart slammed into her throat.

No. Not Red. Anything but Red. She'd rather lose every barrel race next year than lose her mare, her best friend who never judged her.

"What the hell happened to Red?" She started down the steps, but her crutches threw her off-balance. One slipped out from under her. She tried to right herself, bracing her weight against her injured leg. Her knee gave a painful pulse, and a cry escaped her lips. Flailing her arms, she lurched forward—

And felt Ty's strong arm wrap around her waist right before she face-planted in the dirt.

"Damn it, Ella." Ty pulled her close so her back pressed firmly against his chest, bracing her body against his.

His hand was warm, his palm pressing against a sliver of skin revealed between the bottom of her tank and the top of her shorts.

She could feel his heart beating against her back.

Heat—slow, simmering, and seductive—worked from every point his body touched hers to her belly. His touch tantalizing every nerve in her body.

Horrified, she pushed away, righting herself on her crutches.

As though reading her mind, Ty pulled his hand away, shoving it deep in his back pocket. His expression went instantly from concerned to shuttered.

Part of her wanted to process what just happened, but now was not the time.

"Where's my horse?" Her voice came out low, dangerous. If anything happened to Red—

Ty pulled his hands from his pockets, showing his palms. "She's back at the Rocking H. I noticed she was limping this morning, and I want to keep an eye on her."

Okay, the pain medications were clearly making her hallucinate. There was no other reason to explain how this situation continued to go from bad to worse. "I'm sorry. What did you just say?"

Ty swallowed, his Adam's apple bobbing. "She's limping. Based on my early assessment, it looks like she may have injured her flexor tendon. It looks swollen and hot, and I thought it best to not put her into a trailer immediately."

"You can't be serious." Blood rushed in her ears, blocking the sound of her voice. She couldn't tell if she spoke the words at a normal volume or yelled them.

Judging by the way Ty suddenly braced himself, she had yelled them.

The pounding in her head intensified, and it felt like the world was tipping on its axis.

This couldn't be possible. Her horse, her partner in crime, the reason she was even competitive this season was also injured.

"Ella?"

She couldn't handle the concern in his voice. The pity. She was so sick of pity. Everyone had stopped feeling bad for her once she started winning, and she didn't want to go back to that place.

"How the hell did my horse get injured? Didn't Colton cool her down?" The accusation dripped from her voice, but she couldn't help it. Her brain refused to accept the fact Red could be injured. She needed something—or someone—to blame.

"Whoa." Ty held up both hands. "Colton is not to blame. Either the accident or the race caused the injury. We noticed a minor tick in her walk last night, so I had him wrap her legs before the trip home. My hope was it was minor and wouldn't flare into something bigger. Unfortunately, that's not the case."

"But she was fine when we left," she insisted. She saw her horse herself.

Ty crossed his arms over his broad chest, the muscles of his exposed forearms flexing as a storm crossed over his face.

"You will not blame Colton for an accident that was out of our control. Sometimes these injuries take hours to show." His voice was sharp. Any sense of friendliness he had shown earlier had quickly faded. "I didn't drive Red over as a favor to you, so we didn't risk further injury. I can keep her at the Rocking H for the time being and set up a therapy and recovery plan for her. But I can't do that without your permission."

Dear god, leave it Ty to come in yet again and try to save the day. It was like the guy never heard no from anyone.

She didn't need saving. She'd take care of her horse herself. More than anything, she wanted her mare here, with her, where she could keep her own eye on her.

"She will not be staying at the Rocking H." There was no way she'd leave her horse on someone else's ranch, much less the Rocking H. Her father would be beyond furious. He always said to never trust a Hartman.

And she knew better than to trust Ty.

"The Rocking H is an ideal place for her to stay so I can watch her," Ty said in that calm, collected voice that grated against her nerves.

"I don't think so." She gripped her crutches and tried to pull herself to her full five foot five. Ty still towered over her by at least six inches.

"You should consider—"

"Red is better off at home where I can keep an eye on her," she insisted. "You will get her back here."

Ty's jaw jutted forward, and dark red spots formed above his sharp cheekbones. "You absolutely will not choose pride over your horse's well-being."

She blinked. Ty may as well have slapped her.

"I'm not sure if it's a tendon pull or strain, but she needs to be somewhere where a vet can keep an eye on her and run her through therapy every day. She's on my ranch, I'm a vet, and I have the equipment necessary to care for her. Let's not forget you are out of commission yourself. What are you going do to? Watch your horse do her own therapy?"

The frustrating man had a point, but she was too upset to care. One afternoon gone wrong, and now she was watching her future swirl down the drain.

"What's in it for you?" She crossed her arms and stared at him. From her experience, no one offered help unless there was something in it for them.

Ty's face tightened, his jaw clenched so tight, a muscle ticked. "What's in it for me? Nothing. I'm a vet. Your horse is injured. I'm here to help the animal."

She didn't quite believe him, but she let her arms drop to her side. She needed Red to recover as soon as possible, but how much would it cost? The treatment was likely expensive, and the only place that money could come from was the down payment she'd been saving. She'd pay the money if she had to, but there had to be a better way.

Ty scowled at her silence. She waited for him to throw out another barb, but instead he jerked his thumb at the dark mare behind him. "Has this horse been fed?"

Mickey, the four-year-old mare Ella had bought this past spring with the intent of starting her barrel horse training program, had her head stretched out toward the haystack. Her chest pressed firmly against the fencing wire, and her large, square teeth were exposed as she tried to nip in some hay.

"I've got it," Ella sighed. She started slowly down the porch.

"Don't bother," Ty grunted, the annoyance still clear in his voice. He set the foil baking pan on the porch railing.

"I said—" But Ty was already heading toward the stack. A few minutes later, Mickey was happily munching away on breakfast, and Ty was heading up the porch.

"Don't make a decision now," Ty said curtly. "Call me when you've cooled down, and I will drive you out to see Red. Maybe then we can have a rational conversation as to if the horse should stay at Rocking H or not."

She swallowed as Ty narrowed his eyes at her.

"If you threw my card away, you can google my office number." And with that, he spun on his heel and marched back to his truck, his back ramrod straight.

Stunned, she stood on the porch, the crutches digging painfully into her arms as she watched him back out of her driveway and then disappear toward downtown.

She stared at the baking pan on her porch railing and slowly turned toward the door to her trailer. She wasn't a bad guy for wanting to keep her horse on her property to make sure the mare was healing right, but Ty just made her feel like the biggest jerk on the planet. And she hated the whisper in the back of her mind that he just might be right.

CHAPTER FOUR

ELLA'S EYES FELT gritty from crying, and she was annoyed at herself for giving way to tears. But between being cooped up on the couch, her body aching, and accepting the fact that her dream was likely on hold, tears were bound to happen.

Ty implying she cared more about her pride, and her career, than her horse really tipped her over the edge.

"I'm sure he didn't mean it that way," Jordan said as she wandered into the kitchen, cocking her head at the foil tray. "Who brought this over?"

After Ty left, she'd called Jordan to let her know she was alive and home. Jordan came over before her shift at the hospital started, her hair up in a tight bun and wearing blue loose-fitting scrubs.

"I don't know. I know rumors fly quickly in a small town, but I got injured and less than twenty-four hours later food shows up at my place? It had to be someone who tracks rodeo."

"Or a neighbor?" Jordan was already peeling back the foil, revealing an apple crisp. "Oh damn. This smells like heaven on earth. Can I have a bite? I have a long shift ahead of me."

The other woman was already heading for the utensil drawer before Ella could respond.

"Go for it. I don't trust strange food. That could be poisoned."

"Strange food?" Jordan dug right in without a concern. "This is Garnet Valley. Neighbors make dishes for people who need help all the time."

"Not for me they don't," she said drily. No one had ever sent her food before. So while it may be normal for Jordan, and apparently Ty, it was odd for her. Her neighbors would have stopped by and knocked.

"Have you called your parents?" Jordan stabbed her fork into the apples and crumbled topping and took a huge bite.

Ella's mouth watered as the scent of sweet apples and cinnamon wafted over to her.

"Oh dear god," Jordan groaned. "That's one good crisp. I hope you find out who made it. I'd pay them to make me another."

Her stomach growled.

Maybe after Jordan left, she'd have a bite, though she was still plenty suspicious of the anonymous sender. Why not leave a note?

"Dad reacted as expected, and it took me twenty minutes to convince him that he didn't need to come back to help out while I was injured," Ella said, answering Jordan's earlier question. Though to be honest, every part of her wanted him to come take care of her and ease some weight from her mind. "He has that new hardware store he manages, and I don't want to interfere with his success. He's doing well. And Mom just got a job at a bookstore she loves."

The last thing she wanted to do was pull her father away from his work now that he finally had his feet under him. She was proud of him for making the move and finding success at a job. His voice sounded lighter, and he laughed more.

She couldn't bring him back here. Even if it was to take care of her for a few weeks.

Jordan went to the freezer, rummaged around, and came back to the counter with a carton of vanilla ice cream. She and Jordan had been friends for so long that the other woman moved around her kitchen like it was her own.

"I'm glad to hear they're doing so well. I know the move to Oregon was a big decision for them." Her friend grabbed a bowl and waved it at her. "Are you sure you don't want any?"

Her stomach grumbled insistently. "Positive."

Jordan shrugged and scooped some crisp into the bowl and topped it with a large scoop of ice cream. "Did you tell them about Red?"

Ella swallowed and eased onto a stool at the kitchen island. The cheap laminate countertop was cool against her bare arms. Her leg felt stiff and heavy strapped into a brace, and she shifted her butt to the edge of the seat so the weight of her leg and brace wasn't hanging from her hip.

"I didn't dare tell him. He was in a good mood, and he would have blown a gasket. Dad is still bitter Beau Hartman took our horses, and he's adamant that Beau calling in the debt was unfair."

Jordan held up her hands. "I'm not getting into the middle of that one." She paused and chewed an apple thoughtfully. "So, are you going to do it? Leave Red with Ty?"

Her head hadn't stopped pounding since she woke up, and this thing with Red wasn't making it any better. This was the third time in three days Ty had come to her rescue. The dance, the rodeo, and now Red.

And she wasn't the type that needed, or wanted, rescuing.

Unfortunately, Ty had a point about her horse traveling.

"I'd rather Red be here so I can keep an eye on her, but if she's as bad as Ty thinks, it probably isn't wise to put her in a trailer and take her down that worn, pitted highway back to my place." She pressed her hands against her cheeks. "I would have preferred it was anyone but Ty. I don't know what's in it for him."

"Why would there need to be something in it for him?"

Ella rolled her eyes. "Because he and his dad took and sold my rodeo horse? Or because he and Jeff are friends?" Though he had stuck up for her at the rodeo dance. "And I've already learned that Jeff was only interested in me for his own self-serving interests."

"Hmm…" Her friend didn't look convinced. "I don't think Ty and Jeff are friends anymore. I heard they had a falling out a couple years ago."

Ella straightened on her seat. She had not been aware of that. Those two had been as thick as thieves growing up and into college. She shifted. Maybe that was why Ty didn't mind sticking up for her at the dance.

"Besides," Jordan continued. "He's got a reputation as the best vet in the valley for a reason. And I don't think it's because there's something in it for him."

"You mean besides recognition, a larger reputation, and more clients?" Ella listed off, ticking her fingers. "Red is famous in Montana right now, and I can see Ty taking advantage of this opportunity."

"Look." Jordan pointed her fork at Ella. "You need to think about how wise it is for Red to be here. You're injured and don't have the knowledge to work on Red's therapy."

"You could help," Ella threw out there.

"One, I'm an expert in human health care, not animal health care. Two, you know I'm going out of town in the next couple of days for that medical conference. Where does that leave you?"

Helpless at home. Ella dug her fingers into her hairline and pressed. She needed to figure out how to feed, how to cook, heck, even how to get around town while she was on crutches and pain medication.

And she also had to determine if her dream of going to the NFR and buying a small ranch this year was even salvageable.

She dropped her head between her hands. "I could ask my neighbors."

"I have no doubt Ms. Minna will make dinner for you every night, but we both know that she is not going to work your horse," Jordan said, her voice firm. "Besides your father's grudge, and the fact he and Jeff were friends, what is your issue with Ty?"

She worked her jaw.

"I just don't trust him," she said finally. "Ty Hartman fooled me, and Jeff Parker fooled me. I'm not going to be fooled again, and certainly not by the same man twice."

Jordan looked like she wanted to say something but stopped herself.

"Spit it out," Ella said.

"We aren't in high school anymore, and the man has grown up. He's a good vet, and he's going to give it to you straight. If he says Red is better off at his place, there isn't a reason you shouldn't trust him. I'm not going to force you to keep your horse there, but if you want to up your chances to get back into the rodeo circuit as soon as possible, I'd leave your mare at Ty's."

Ella drummed her fingers against the cheap kitchen island, studying her friend.

"I looked at your standings this morning," Jordan continued. "While you and Lindsey were neck-in-neck at the beginning of the season, you've pulled ahead significantly. You still have a chance to qualify for Finals."

So there was a chance she could go to the NFR. Ella had been too afraid to even look at the standings. She already knew that if she had been able to keep going this season, her route to the NFR was practically guaranteed. Maybe, just maybe, her season wasn't quite over yet.

"I'm out for eight to ten weeks," Ella pointed out. "That gives Lindsey plenty of time to catch up, to qualify ahead of me. Add on Red's injury... You wouldn't happen to have a horse I could borrow again?"

Jordan laughed at the reference. Ella had borrowed a barrel horse from Jordan during high school after her dad gave her mare, Rocky, to Beau to pay off the debt. "I'd lend you my cutting horse, but I don't think Quinn would know what to do with a barrel."

She laughed, but it sounded hollow. How had she tumbled from the crest of success to the valley floor down below? "Shit."

Her friend came around the counter and pulled Ella into a hug.

"There's no way that Lindsey won't take the lead." And it killed her that Lindsey of all people was going to take her place at the Finals. Lindsey who had friended her in high school only to mess with her head. "And Ty sees this as an opportunity."

Jordan shook her head. "Ty saved you from two drunk cowboys, one who used to be his friend. He also took you to the hospital after you got injured, drove you home, and offered to take care of Red."

There had to be something he had his eye on. The question was what?

"He probably feels obligated to help out."

"Or maybe Ty isn't as terrible as you think he is," Jordan said quietly.

No, that wasn't true. She had learned her lesson from Lindsey, from Ty, from Jeff—none of them wanted anything to do with her until she started being successful.

"Do you think I'm more concerned with my career and pride than I am with Red?" she asked, voicing the concern Ty had put in her head.

Jordan shook her head. "I think you're in a shitty situation and trying to do what's best for you and your horse. Unfortunately, the best thing may be to leave her with someone you'd rather avoid."

Leave it to Jordan to say it as it was.

"I'll consider leaving Red at Rocking H," she relented. But that didn't mean she trusted Ty.

ON INFREQUENT DAYS off from his vet practice, Ty used the time to catch up on ranch repairs and management.

"That ought to do it," Ty said as Jace placed the end cap on a wheel line where a section of pipe had sprung a leak. They wheeled the pipe section over to the pickup and loaded it into the truck bed before walking to the other end of the line to turn the water back on.

The damp stalks of alfalfa brushed against Ty's jeans until the denim was soaked through, and the irrigated ground was soft under his boots. He ducked his head against the slight chill in the wind. Soon enough it would be jacket weather again.

Ty twisted the valve to the waterline open and listened to the rush of water flowing into the wheel line followed by the heavy *thunk* as the flow hit each sprinkler head, bringing the wheel line back to life.

The two brothers ducked out of the way of the end sprinkler head as it shot water in a wide arch directed at them. Jace had done this enough now to know to get out of the way. The first time they had gone out to move wheel lines, his brother had ended up soaked from head to foot.

"What do you do with the broken pipe?" Jace asked as they climbed into the ancient rig, settling onto the old cloth seats. The truck doors creaked as they slammed them shut.

"I'll see if I can repair it," Ty said as he pointed the truck back to the ranch, driving slowly over the worn path along the edge of the field to avoid creating ruts. "One day, I'd like to get a pivot on this field so we aren't constantly replacing worn-out pipe. Plus, they're more water efficient than wheel line. Win-win."

Transitioning the ranch from wheel line to pivot was a long-distant goal, though. First things first, he needed to focus on making sure the ranch stayed in the family, and after that, he would shift his vet practice to Rocking H.

Jace nodded and stared out the window. "You know, I never would have guessed I'd spend a year in Montana on a ranch. Then when I got here, I never thought I'd enjoy this. Now I think I'll miss this when our time is up. I can see how the life grows on you."

Ty's stomach dropped like a rock in a pond. "Decided already, huh?"

Jace let out a soft laugh. "Come on, man. What am I going to do here? Mine and Hailey's life is in Houston. I have a new building that will start construction right when I get back. My aunt lives there. Hailey has contracts there. We have no ties to this place."

"It's your legacy. It's part of your family." The second he said the words, he knew it was the wrong thing to say. Jace went rigid, and the mood of the cab dimmed.

"No, Ty, it's *your* legacy. It's Colton's legacy. You guys grew up around this. Lived this. Breathed this." Jace motioned out of the truck window at the broad expanse of land that rolled out in endless waves. "It was never mine. The old man left me in Houston without a second thought. He knew I didn't belong here. Even I know I'm out of my element here."

That wasn't entirely true. Sure, Jace had been out of his comfort zone when he had first arrived. However, Ty and

Colton had done everything they could to make sure Jace felt involved in the ranch, learned the ropes, and figured out the ins and outs.

He had wanted Jace to feel like he had some control and ownership in the ranch. And his efforts had paid off as Jace grew more and more confident each day. The guy didn't hesitate when he was around horses and cows anymore, and he frequently started the morning chores before he and Colton were out.

"It's in your blood," Ty insisted. "You're adapting quickly. You look like you belong here."

Jace snorted derisively. "Right. Now that I have your old Levi's?" Jace refused to wear Wranglers. "Adapting or not, this place was never mine. I'm living at the home of a father that didn't want me, and my life is back in Texas. I'll come visit, but we both know that Montana doesn't fit."

It wasn't rational, and he knew it wasn't rational, but learning that Jace wasn't planning to stick around was making him feel ill, out of control.

Abandoned.

Again.

It took everything he had to not hit the brakes, lock the doors, and hash everything out until Jace agreed that this ranch was his legacy as well. He wanted to ask Jace to stay, but suddenly felt like he was seventeen again and trying to convince his mom to stay in Montana.

She hadn't bothered to stick around. So why would Jace?

"What do you plan—" Ty started but was cut short when he spotted a white truck parked in front of the barn.

Garnet Valley was small enough that he recognized most trucks, and Jordan's white pickup with a dent in the front bumper was hard to miss.

His eyes landed on the two women in the front seat.

Jordan. And Ella.

His question for Jace evaporated on his tongue.

Jordan had her eyes on him as he parked the ancient ranch truck by the barn. Ella, on the other hand, was looking at the ranch as though she had never been on the property before. Her eyes were as wide as silver dollars.

Granted, the last time she was on the Rocking H was years ago and likely before it had fallen into disrepair.

"Who's that?" Jace asked.

"The woman who owns Red," he said shortly, pushing the rusty truck door open. The damp denim of his jeans felt cold and clammy against his skin, and he would love to change into a dry pair, but there was no way he was going to disappear inside the ranch house to change with Ella on the property. He didn't trust that she wouldn't load up Red and disappear down the road.

"I see," Jace said as though he understood perfectly.

Ty slammed the heavy door behind him as Jordan hopped out of her rig. Ella pushed her door open and took her time getting out.

"I didn't realize you two were coming by." Ty drawled out the words watching Ella's reaction carefully.

"We called, but you didn't answer," Ella bit out as she pulled sunglasses over her eyes then maneuvered her leg out of the truck.

Even with dark sunglasses, but he could tell her complexion was still too pale. Her long hair was pulled back into a long braid over her shoulder, a few strands escaping to frame her face. It made her look soft and vulnerable.

Only he knew better than to be deceived by Ella's appearance.

He held out his hand, stepping closer, but Ella quickly waved him away.

"I've got it." Grabbing the "oh shit" handle on her side, she eased herself down, landing on her good leg, and keeping her weight off the other.

He held up both hands and took a step back as she reached into the backseat and grabbed her crutches.

If she didn't want help, he wasn't going to force it on her.

"After our call went to voicemail, we figured we could drive out and try to find you," Jordan offered.

Ella's mouth was pulled tight, and he could tell that she wasn't pleased to be there. She kept looking around, pausing at the herds of cows and horses that were now a tiny fraction of their original size. His shoulders hunched forward as Ella continued to say nothing.

"Where's Red?" she asked finally, pulling her gaze back to him.

"Right around here," he said, motioning to the side of the barn. It probably would have been easier for Jordan to drive her over, but Ella tucked her chin and started moving in the direction he'd pointed.

She wore jean cutoff shorts, exposing her long, lean, tan legs, and the threads escaping the raw hem of her shorts brushed against her thighs as she swung herself along the uneven path, the muscles in her legs flexing with each move.

Was there a part of this woman that wasn't gorgeous?

Jordan fell in step with him and cleared her throat.

He quickly averted his eyes, pulling his gaze to a spot just beyond Ella's shoulder.

"Question for you," Jordan said, keeping her voice low. "I'm heading out for a conference in a couple days, and I worry about her." The woman jerked her head in the direction of Ella who was gaining ground as both he and Jordan slowed their pace. "Would you mind keeping an eye on her? If you are already taking care of Red, you can also keep tabs on her without her really knowing."

Tilting his head back, he closed his eyes against the glare of sun. "Jordan—"

"Just throwing it out there. You and I both know that Ella doesn't like to give many people a chance."

"And I'm no exception," he muttered. Where the hell had Jordan even got this crazy idea? "She's not going to go for it. And, honestly, I'm not up for it. Being her vet is the best I can do for her."

Jordan sighed, and he thought that was the end of the conversation.

"Just think about it," Jordan said. "She's on her own."

And he hated that she was on her own and hurting, but there was no way he was going to involve himself more in her life. Ella wanted him out of her way, and after their last encounter, he was more than happy to oblige.

But the damn request burrowed in the back of his brain.

He glanced up at Ella just as she approached the pen containing her mare.

The second Ella caught sight of her horse, he sensed, rather than saw, the tension ease from her body. Just like that, the barbed wire and careful barriers she had in place melted away.

"Hey there, girl," Ella crooned. She pushed her sunglasses to the top of her head then held out her hand.

Red nickered a greeting as she swung her big, anvil-shaped head over the railing and pressed her muzzle into Ella's palm.

Ella's face softened. The look of determination, the press of her lips, even the edge of her jaw, relaxed into an open expression of love.

Even if he wanted to, there was no way he could tear his eyes away from her. Her entire demeanor had shifted to easy, open, and gentle.

A sliver of regret threaded through him. It was only this morning that he accused her of caring more about her pride than her horse. Looking at her now, he was clearly in the wrong. The escaped strands of her hair blew in the wind as she pressed her face against the white snip at the end of her horse's nose.

This was a side of Ella he never saw. Around him, it was all barriers and barbs and walls. This side of her was…stunning.

A warm pull stirred low in his belly, like a gravitational force, and he found himself fighting to keep from drawing nearer.

Not wise, the rational part of his brain advised. The irrational part of his body wanted to touch her, draw her close.

He shoved his hands deep in his front pockets.

"It's her front leg, right by the cannon bone," he said, retreating to the safety of veterinary medicine. It was either that or say something stupid. Ella was on edge enough around him without adding his conflicting feelings to the mix.

"I see that," Ella said as her eyes dropped to the vet-wrapped bandages around both of her horse's slender forelegs before her gaze ran along the rest of Red's body, carefully assessing her horse, looking for other injuries. "What's the recovery time you expect?"

Ty stepped cautiously closer. He freed his hands from his pockets and gripped the fence railing. "If it's a minor strain, six to eight weeks."

"Similar to me," Ella said, a hopeful note in her voice.

"But if it's severe, eight to ten months."

Her entire body seemed to droop. The light in her eyes diminished, and her mouth pulled down hard in the corners. "Months? Eight to ten *months*? That's almost a year!"

He nodded slowly, keeping eye contact with her to show just how serious he was. "I would recommend an ultrasound to determine how serious the injury is. It will let us plan accordingly. However, I already suspect that it will take at least three months for her to recover and be ready to train again. So maybe four months until she's fully recovered and racing."

"Why didn't you do an ultrasound earlier?" she asked. It wasn't a condemnation. She just sounded stunned, confused. He could practically read it in her face. Two hits to her rodeo career within twenty-four hours. Ella had to be reeling.

And for some damn reason, he wanted to steady her.

"I normally don't do a procedure on an animal without the

owner's permission, and you weren't exactly willing to talk when I stopped by this morning. I gave her an anti-inflammatory and iced her for a bit this morning to help the swelling go down."

Ella's gaze flitted back to Red before she ducked her head. "Shit. Okay." There was a catch in her voice, and he could see the chords of her neck move as she swallowed. "I don't have a couple months. The Finals are in three months. Is there anything we can do?"

"An ultrasound. Followed by a routine to reduce the swelling. Once the swelling is down, and we confirm everything looks good, we start with light exercise and therapy to get the tendon back in order." He dropped his head and rubbed at the back of his neck. "We essentially take this day by day. Hopefully, it's a light tear and it's a quick recovery. If it's a larger tear than expected…"

Ella's body went eerily still. Then slowly she turned toward him, her entire body rigid, as though she were waiting for him to sucker punch her. "Why do I get the feeling I'm not going to like this?"

He sucked in a breath. "Recovery isn't guaranteed if the injury is severe."

She was shaking her head before he could even finish. Her eyes were wide, too wide, as she opened her mouth to say something, but nothing came out.

This was his chance. "If we add in pressure point therapy, it could help reduce the recovery time by a few weeks or more, and possibly help her recover from a more severe injury. If the injury isn't too severe, she could be running by the time Finals comes around. Not her best run, but you could make a show-ing."

Sucking in her lip, Ella bit down until it was white.

Placing a possessive hand on Red's neck, she turned away from him. "Is this my fault? For…" she waved her hand, as though trying to come up with the words. "…for delaying anything?"

He wished he had never told her she was too proud to care for her horse.

As a vet, he knew people were tied to their animals, their lives intricately woven. It was the nature of growing up in a place like Montana. Animals were a part of your life, and they left their brands on the hearts of their humans.

"Hey."

She flinched at his voice and turned farther away.

"You didn't delay anything. I did the same thing with her I would have done with any horse." He moved closer, wanting to give her comfort, but not quite sure how. Ella always appeared to be so strong, he didn't know how this more vulnerable side of her would react to comfort.

He reached out and squeezed her shoulder.

His fingers hit her soft bare skin exposed by the strap of her black tank. A bolt of warm shot through him. If she felt the same, it didn't show.

"She's going to be fine. But she needs to stay at the ranch, where I can keep an eye on her and put her on a recovery schedule. I do not recommend loading her in a trailer and taking her down the dirt roads and unmaintained highway to your place until she is ready. And right now, Red isn't ready."

Ella glanced over her shoulder at him. Her lips were less than an inch from where his fingers rested on her shoulder. A long, teasing strand of dark hair fell across one eye as she looked to him for confirmation.

"What I said back at your place, what I implied, it was wrong. I'm sorry I made you worry. I know you care about Red more than anything. I've watched you two at rodeos, and I know you're a team."

Ella nodded. He could feel her breath on his hand, and he didn't want to move away.

Jordan cleared her throat, and he dropped his hand like he'd been burned. For a minute there, he'd forgotten they weren't alone.

Ella turned back to her horse. "So this pressure point therapy... You think it will really work."

"I don't have a doubt in my mind." Everything he read and studied showed significant results.

"Are you sure you aren't doing this because you'll get the recognition if it does work?" she asked. Her voice didn't hold an accusation.

He shook his head. Sure, if the recovery went well, this would help boost his reputation, but as always, his focus was on the animal first and foremost. And he was positive this therapy would be the way to go.

After a moment, Ella pulled her shoulders back, lifted her chin, and set her expression. "Fine. She can stay here. You can do the therapy. But I want to be here every time the therapy happens."

"It'll be about three to four times a week," he pointed out, so she knew how much time she'd be spending with him.

"I'm willing to commit to it," she agreed.

For a minute, he could only stare. Had she really just agreed to his idea? He glanced back at Jace, who was smiling as he leaned against the fence, his eyes on the famous horse.

"Deal." He held out his hand.

Ella looked at it warily, before pressing her palm against his. He tried to ignore the surge of desire that laced through him at the innocent contact. But the blush high on Ella's cheekbones made it impossible to ignore the reaction.

She felt it too.

"Deal," Ella said, her voice just a touch throatier than it had been a minute ago.

CHAPTER FIVE

T HE NEXT DAY, Ella awoke to knocking at her front door.

"What the—?" She pulled her cell phone off her worn nightstand and squinted at the time.

It was past seven. A late wake-up for her, but too early for visitors.

The knocking stopped. Ella pushed the sheets to the top of her thighs, allowing the cool morning air to caress her skin.

The hammering at her door started again.

"One minute," she yelled.

Whoever it was had better be going through a life-or-death crisis to wake her up this early.

Rubbing the sleep out of her eyes, she grabbed her crutches, and eased herself out of bed.

"For the love of god—" Ella yanked the door open, and stared at Jordan, who was in her scrubs with two baking dishes in her hand. She gave her friend a sheepish smile.

Jordan hoisted the two large baking pans in her arms. "You're such a grouch in the mornings. I'm leaving tonight for the conference, and I wanted to drop these off."

Ella stepped back so her friend could walk in. "You're too good to me," she said, feeling chagrined.

"I know." Jordan set both dishes on the counter. "You're

lucky I don't mind your morning grumpiness. Did I wake you?"

"No." She scrubbed her hand down her face as her fuzzy brain tried to work without caffeine. "Yes."

Her friend's brows knitted together as she turned to look over her shoulder. "Then who fed your horse?"

"Mickey?" Ella struggled out the front door, stopped on her porch, and squinted against the morning light. Sure enough, the mare was happily munching away at the flakes of hay piled in the wheel trough.

There was also a mug of coffee on her porch step, the closed lid keeping it warm.

There was no way Ms. Minna had fed the horse. Her sweet seventy-something neighbor had certainly brought a pie over the second she saw Ella on crutches, but there was no way she'd engage in manual labor. Despite living in Montana her entire life, Ms. Minna was not a fan of horses. Mrs. Thompson, the neighbor on the other side who typically fed her horses while she was out of town, was still away visiting family.

"You didn't feed my horses?" She inspected her friend's blond hair for telltale leaves or stalks of alfalfa. Heaven knew she couldn't feed without getting hay in her hair.

Jordan shook her head. "Nope. Mickey was fed when I showed up. By the way, I brought some groceries to hold you over for a few days while I'm away. You may have to ask Ms. Minna to take you on her shopping trip if you can't drive yet—"

There was no way she'd go grocery shopping with Ms. Minna. Her neighbor treated the trip to the store as an afternoon event that involved stopping to gossip with everyone in the store and wandering up and down every aisle. Yes, it was cute, but there was no way that she'd be up to enduring the endless shopping trip.

Jordan went to her truck, talking the whole time while Ella continued to stare warily at her horse. Her eyes slid to the coffee mug on her porch railing. The name of Ty's vet practice was scrawled across the front of the blue mug.

Where did Ty get the idea she needed help with her horse?

Jordan slammed her truck door and carried two plastic bags up the porch steps and dropped them inside.

"As for the casseroles," Jordan continued. "You can heat them up at 350 in the oven, and—"

Jordan stopped short as she took in Ella's expression.

"Jordan, I love you and you're my best friend, but do you know anything about Ty Hartman stopping by to feed my horse?"

Her friend slowly shook her head, her eyes a bit too wide and a bit too innocent.

"And you didn't happen to mention to him you were going out of town tonight, did you?"

Jordan shrugged. "I may have mentioned it."

Ella rubbed at the back of her neck. Meddling friends…

"The last thing I need is Ty ending up in one more area of my life. Isn't it enough that he's working with Red? Now he has to stop by and feed my horse every day?"

"If you want to be actively involved in Red's care, he has to stop by anyway," Jordan pointed out, ever practical. "Besides, who else is going to take care of you while I'm gone?"

"Me?" Ella curled her fingers to her chest. "I'll take care of me."

"Besides, I think Ty may have a thing for you. Maybe if you two spent some time together—"

"Don't even go there," Ella warned. Things between her and Ty were already tricky. The fact that she was going to spend time with him as he tried this new therapy only made it more complicated. There was no way she was going to give in to any attraction to him.

"I think the man has it bad," Jordan whispered.

A little thrill of victory raced through her body, and she quickly suppressed it. Nothing was going to happen between them. End of story.

"You need to stop that fantasy dead in its tracks," Ella ground out, trying to ignore the knowing look on her friend's face. It made her feel exposed, like her friend was cracking open her soul and revealing a secret.

"Ty is the last man on earth who wants anything to do with me, and honestly, after Jeff, I'm done with privileged cowboys from Western Montana. They are all the same." Ty had shown his hand once in high school and then a second time when his family left her family horseless. She wasn't playing that hand again only to find out that Ty was just the same as Jeff.

"Do you really think Ty is arrogant?" Jordan asked quietly.

Ella opened her mouth, ready to argue with Jordan's question, but stopped when Jordan's mouth tightened.

She carefully rolled through the events of the past few days, trying to come up with an example. He was direct, quiet, honest, and upfront. But he hadn't been arrogant.

She shifted uncomfortably and looked away.

"I think you should give him a chance," Jordan said. She grabbed the coffee from the porch and set it inside next to the casseroles. "I don't think it would hurt."

Jordan headed out shortly after with a promise to check in every day.

She on the other hand was on leave until the doctor gave her the all-clear to work. At first, the idea of having a few days off from waitressing seemed like a dream.

She should have known better. With Jordan's words in her head, it was hard to sit still.

Maybe she had misjudged Ty.

The thought didn't sit well. After all, she knew what it was like to be judged based on circumstances, and she had been doing that very thing to him.

It didn't seem…fair.

A few hours later, she was still stewing on it.

He had apologized to her yesterday; maybe it was her turn to say something in return. At the very least they could settle into some sort of truce. It would probably make their agreement with Red easier. If she were going to start eating into her savings to make sure Red recovered as quickly as possible, the least she could do was play ball and not make things any tougher on them.

Maybe if she and Ty were on better terms, those pesky butterfly feelings she got whenever he was around would finally go away.

It was driving her nuts that she didn't know what to expect from him. She thought she had his character nailed down, but she'd begun to doubt herself. Maybe Ty had grown up and changed? She'd hate to think she'd been going on faulty information this whole time. Either way, life was much easier when they avoided each other.

By late afternoon, she was bored of sitting around and ready to climb the walls. The idea of apologizing to Ty made her feel off, and there were only so many naps to take and movies she could watch. Even her favorite movies didn't distract her from Ty.

When the knock at the door came, she practically sprang off the couch and would have raced to the door if she wasn't hindered by her crutches.

Glancing at her window, she spotted Ms. Minna with another pie in her hands.

"Ms. Minna," Ella greeted her elderly neighbor enthusiastically. Ms. Minna made the best pie in town, hands down.

"Hi, honey." The older woman's olive skin folded into a multitude of wrinkles as she smiled. They had a long history together. Ms. Minna had babysat Ella when she was a kid, and as Ella grew into a teen and then an adult, she would help with her neighbor's chores. "I brought you another pie."

"You know I love your pie," Ella said, pushing the door open to let her neighbor in.

Before Ms. Minna could cross the threshold, a big blue truck pulled up just outside her driveway. Ty sat behind the wheel, looking as handsome as ever.

That annoying fluttery feeling started again, and she could feel the heat rising to her cheeks.

Ms. Minna looked over her shoulder, and then turned back to wink at Ella as the long-legged cowboy climbed out of the truck. The man walked like he had all the time in the world—easy, slow strides that ate up lengths of ground with each step.

"Oh, it's that handsome vet again. He's been stopping by a lot lately." The older woman tilted her head. "Are you two seeing each other?"

Ms. Minna's voice seemed to echo off every trailer in the neighborhood. There was no way Ty didn't hear.

"No," she said quickly and loudly.

"Well, he isn't getting the memo because that boy just keeps stopping by." Ms. Minna leaned close. "If I were you, I'd go for it. He's got this sexy, stoic vet vibe going on, you know what I mean? Do you want me to ask him for you?"

The late afternoon sun suddenly felt about ten degrees too hot. Her hair was up in the same ponytail she had slept in and she hadn't bothered with makeup. At least she was in a black tank dress instead of worn-out shorts this time.

Ella heard the sound of cowboy boots on her porch steps, and she didn't dare look up.

No doubt her face had covered every shade of red imaginable as Ms. Minna grinned up at her as though they were sharing a secret.

All she could do was stare back at her long-time neighbor.

"Hi, Ty," Ms. Minna said when Ella couldn't get her voice to work. "I was just talking about you. I was saying—"

That kicked her into gear. She looked up, and suddenly she understood what Ms. Minna meant by sexy, stoic vet. Ty's eyes were serious as he took them both in, his brows slightly lowered, as though he were evaluating the situation. The only sign that he'd overheard her neighbor was one corner of his mouth was ever-so-slightly turned up.

He was amused.

And it was sexy.

How had she missed his sense of humor after all these years?

Maybe Jordan was right.

She sucked in a sharp breath, desperate to get herself out of this embarrassing predicament. So she blurted out the first words that came to mind.

"Are you feeding my horse?" So much for an apology. The words came out as a demand rather than a question.

She could have smacked herself.

Ty jerked back but quickly recovered. At least he was no longer doing that sexy smile thing anymore. That made him far more attractive than any man should be. "Is that a question or an accusation?"

Hell, she didn't know. "A question. It just came out as a demand for an answer." She glanced away, but then forced herself to look back at him. "But I think I deserve to know who is feeding my horse."

"You know what?" Ms. Minna said, looking happily at them both, "I'm going to head out and let you two sort this out. Take your time. I'll just drop this pie inside."

Eye contact with Ty felt impossible as Ms. Minna disappeared inside and came out seconds later to hug Ella goodbye. Then, lowering her voice, she said, "The chemistry between you two…"

Unfortunately, Ms. Minna's lowered voice still carried easily.

Groaning inwardly, Ella waited until her neighbor was down the driveway, past the worn wooden fence, and heading to her own house. She didn't dare look at Ty. It was too damn embarrassing.

There was absolutely zero chemistry between them…that she was willing to admit to.

"Great. I'm not sure what kind of gossip will spread over the next couple weeks," she said to Ty. She forced herself to steel her gaze and face him head-on. "I apologize in advance. Not that it's any of my fault. It absolutely isn't."

IT PRETTY MUCH took all his self-control to not laugh. Ms. Minna was certainly on a roll today, and there was no doubt in Ty's mind she would be sharing all her thoughts and opinions on him and Ella at her next trip to the grocery store.

Ella was still shaking her head, even after they watched Ms. Minna walk through her barren front yard, up the creaking wooden porch steps, and disappear inside the ancient brown and cream trailer house.

He could have sworn he saw the white curtains in Ms. Minna's window twitch. The little old lady was probably watching them with curiosity.

"I'm sure we have both been through worse gossip than that," he said.

Ella flinched. "I've been through enough gossip to last a lifetime. And honestly, no one in their right mind would think we are dating anyway."

She made it sound like they were different species.

He crossed his arms. "Why wouldn't—" He stopped and tried again. "Am I not good enough for you?"

Her sharp gaze met his. Color bloomed high on her cheeks. "Not good enough for me? Ha, ha. Nice joke, Ty." Her words were laced with sarcasm.

When she didn't continue, he lifted his brows at her, refusing to speak until she explained herself.

"No, that's not what I'm saying. What I mean is—" She motioned at him, her hands gesturing toward him. "I mean…" Her voice drifted off as her gaze lowered from his eyes to him lips. Then to his neck where he had undone the top few buttons of his shirt. Her gaze continued down to his forearms, her eyes lingering where he had rolled up the long sleeves of his button-down.

Her throat contracted as she swallowed.

Suppressing a groan, he closed his eyes, blocking the site of her hot gaze from his view.

Ms. Minna had not missed the mark by any means.

The feisty cowgirl just refused to acknowledge it.

She felt it just as much as he did.

"Never mind. That's not why you are here. Did you feed my horse?" She was demanding an answer.

"Yes," he said, opting for simple.

"I've got it handled," she said quickly. But this time he saw it for what it was—she was pushing him away because she was attracted to him.

He made her feel flustered.

"You know, some people say 'thank you' when their neighbor does them a favor."

"Don't patronize me," Ella snapped, the stubborn, independent cowgirl he knew and recognized resurfacing.

"Then stop acting stubborn," he countered, keeping a teasing tone to his voice. "So I fed your horse. I figured you had enough on your plate without trying to figure out how to throw hay over the fence while balancing on one leg. I guarantee that won't go well for you. Who will scrape you off the ground? One of your neighbors who's watching us through their windows right now?"

Ella's eyes were shooting fiery emerald sparks at him.

He held up his hands. "Besides, I wanted to check on your horse here and make sure she's transitioning to being an only child alright."

Horses were herd animals and usually didn't do too well on their own. If her mare wasn't happy, he at least had some means to help figure out a solution.

The fire in her expression lowered from full flame to simmering.

"I've noticed she's pawing at the ground more," Ella admitted, though she looked reluctant. "And she appears to be cribbing at the corner where there are wood boards."

He studied the horse. "I noticed the restlessness this morning. She's probably lonely."

Ella shook her head. "I'll figure something out. Once we know how long Red is out, I can come up with a plan."

"You know, I can help out too. I'm your neighborhood vet, after all." He couldn't keep the bite from his voice.

She held her crutches close to her sides, as though she were trying to protect herself. Tucking her chin close to her chest, she shook her head.

"What are you so afraid of?" he asked, his voice softening like he would do with a frightened horse.

"Just because I'm letting you help me out doesn't mean that you need to fix every problem that comes into my life."

"I want to help."

Ella laughed, the sound short and a bit bitter. "People don't typically try to help me. Not unless there is something in it for them."

And, again, she was wondering what was in it for him. It was driving him up the wall. For a second, he thought about telling her if the pressure point therapy worked, he could use it to grow his practice. However, the cowgirl was so wary of what he would gain from the situation, that he knew she'd take her horse straight home if he told her the full truth. Red was much better off at the Rocking H where he could work with her and keep an eye on her daily.

The wind picked up, pushing her long ponytail over her shoulder. Ella pushed her hair back.

"You know, it's okay to accept help from people. Not everyone is out to get you or to talk behind your back."

She snorted. "Right. People never offered help until I was successful. Excuse me that I'm not welcoming everyone with open arms now that my career is on the line.

"No one helped out when my dad had to sell his horse to pay off your dad. He couldn't help out at any more round-ups, and most people laughed behind his back when he lost his job a couple months later."

He'd forgotten about that. Her father, Jared, had lost his job when the elderly couple who owned the feed store he worked at decided to retire. It hadn't been Jared's fault, but it still was bad timing, nonetheless.

"No one helped us then and don't think I didn't hear people gossip about him, how he couldn't support a family. I had to start working that year just to help us stay afloat."

"I'm not laughing at you," he said softly. The breeze pushed her ponytail in front of her shoulder once more. Without thinking, he reached out, and laced her hair between his finger, letting the long strands run along his hand.

Her chest expanded as she closed her eyes. He wanted to roll her length of hair around his hand until he was cupping the base of her neck, tilting her head back, and kissing her.

And that was the problem. Once he started, once he gave into this endless desire that always seemed to surround him whenever he was around her, he knew he wouldn't be able to stop.

Ella would be the one walking away, and he'd be on his own, once again.

Her head tilted back, her chest arching up and toward him fractionally, but just enough that he wanted to step closer, to take the silent invitation she was offering.

He slid his fingers through her hair, freeing her from his gentle grasp before he took a step back.

"Do you want to see Red this afternoon?" he said, redirecting the conversation.

Confusion crossed her features as she looked at him.

The fire in her eyes settled into something different. Something serious.

Like she was really looking at him for the first time. Whether that was a good thing or not, he didn't know.

"Are you going to keep feeding Mickey?" she asked, her voice suddenly much calmer.

"If you'd like me to. I need to come by to pick you up most days anyway."

Ella nodded, the movement slow and thoughtful before she finally dropped her gaze from him. He found himself releasing a breath he didn't know he was holding.

"Let me think about it," she said.

THE TRIP TO the Rocking H was quiet for the most part. As Ty turned on to the gravel road that led to the ranch, Ella snuck a glance at him.

His gaze was held straight ahead, both hands gripping the steering wheel. Ty was keeping her on her toes, and it made her more defensive than usual.

She had *wanted* him to kiss her. He had been so close she could feel the heat radiating from his body. His hand wrapped in her hair. All she had wanted in that moment was for him to pull her close, drop his head and kiss her.

She was getting weak-kneed. That's all there was too it. One guy shows up and helps her when she needs it, and she goes all googly eyed.

Only it didn't feel like something silly like that. It felt far more intense. Part of it might be because this was one of the first times she'd ever let anyone help her…but there was something else at play. Something she didn't care to analyze at the moment.

She still owed him an apology, but part of her was afraid that if she let her guard down enough to legitimately apologized that the emotions that she'd been dodging would only intensify.

Truth be told, she wasn't ready for that. Especially knowing now that Ty could so easily step away from her when she was so clearly offering herself to him.

Heat flooded her face, and she forced herself to look out the passenger window before Ty caught onto the fact that she was worked up about a kiss that would never happen.

With the exception of yesterday, it had been years since she had been out this way. Her father used to help with the roundups and brandings back when Beau and her dad were on better terms. She'd head out on occasion if more help was needed or if she wanted to get out of their tiny home.

After Beau had suddenly called in her dad's debt, leaving her family in bad shape, her father never quite forgave Beau— or any Hartman for that matter, whether they were involved with the deal or not. As far as her father was aware, all Hartmans were bad news. He probably would have personally ripped Ty from limb to limb if he ever found out about the prom prank.

Ella shifted in her seat, on the edge of asking him about the prank, but stopped.

There didn't seem to be a point in drudging up old history. As Jordan said, they'd both grown up. Even as a minor high school grudge, it still felt like a sliver under her nail. Nothing major, but the pain bothered her when she thought of it.

Ty took a left turn, pulling off the old ribbon of highway onto the dusty dirt road that led to the ranch. The road was banked on either side with waving expanses of alfalfa and wheat fields as they headed farther west and closer to the ranch.

When she had seen the ranch yesterday, she couldn't quite believe it. The ranch buildings were in the process of being renovated, but the portions that were not yet repaired clearly showed worn and dilapidated roofs and walls. They were a far cry from the immaculate buildings she remembered when she last stepped foot on the ranch nearly a decade ago.

As ranch buildings and animals came into view, she could see how the livestock herds were significantly reduced, and the pack of dogs and ranch hands that used to greet them was now just an old, blue-speckled cow dog that trotted out, tongue lolling out the side of his mouth in a happy welcome.

On the way home yesterday, she had wondered if she had imagined the vast changes. Today it was clear that her first impression was indeed reality.

"What happened?" she asked, pressing her hands into her thighs. "It looks…" She tried to find a nice way of putting it. "Run-down."

"Wow, and you think I have no tact," Ty said as he pulled the truck up beside the barn. "Is this too far away from Red? I can pull up closer."

Without waiting for her answer, he reversed course and moved closer to the pen where Red was kept.

"I didn't mean to sound rude. I just…" She searched for

the right words. "Nope, I'm going to pull a Ty. Seriously, what happened?"

Ty's knuckles were white on the steering wheel, and for a moment, she wondered if he was going to answer her.

"Never mind, I didn't mean to pry." But looking at this ranch made her wonder if maybe she had been too quick to put Ty into a category that he didn't belong in.

No, he'd certainly been one of the rich kids back in the day. And he still had this expensive truck and a new vet practice that was successful from what she had heard.

Jordan's word shoved their way to the forefront of her mind.

Ty cleared his throat. "Dad hit some rough times financially. Cow prices tanked, and we planted too early. A late frost killed a good portion of our crops, and we didn't have any way to make up for it. I think he fell into a depression after that. He gave up on ranching—laid everyone off, sold off most of the livestock, and just let everything go."

"This wouldn't happen to be the same year…" She trailed off, the pieces clicking together.

"That we called in your debt? Yep. The old man was pretty desperate at that point. He thought for certain he was going to lose the family ranch. Not that you would know looking at him. Beau had that mask of grump and indifference down pat. I think calling in those debts was his last hope to get some funds to hold us over until we could sell some cows. And then beef prices tanked." Ty hit the brakes, jolting them to a stop at the end of the row of pens.

Why hadn't she known that earlier? It could have changed

the situation. They still would've had to sell their horses and she would have had to start working in order to continue with high school rodeo and to make ends meet. But her dad's feelings toward Beau may have been different if he had known the full situation. At least she'd like to think so.

Then again, she wasn't sure, and it didn't sit well. Maybe she'd been too quick to jump to judgment...although thinking back to the way she's been treated by Ty's friends, she couldn't say for sure. But that was then, and this is now, and like a thorn jammed in her sock, there was something she needed to do to fix it.

"I'm sorry. I had no idea." She pressed her hands against her thighs, curling her fingers under the edge of her denim shorts.

"Don't be. Beau wasn't one to air his problems." As though sensing her tension, Ty placed a hand on top of hers. His pinky finger hit the skin just above the brace. "I've been trying to hold this ranch together, to keep what little of it was left running smoothly, and to not lose it all. It's been hell, and some days I don't see an end in sight." He dropped his head back against the seat. "I don't even know if I can keep the ranch in the family."

This was news to her. Granted she knew that Ty and his brothers would end up with Rocking H, but it never dawned on her that it wouldn't be all sunshine and roses.

Ty's expression looked pinched and drawn as he spoke about the ranch.

It was like pulling back a curtain on the cowboy. She hadn't realized that the ranch was a sore spot or that he was struggling. She wanted to comfort him in some way but didn't know where to begin.

"Should we get out and check on Red?" The words sounded forced as he jerked his thumb toward her mare.

Yes, they should get out of the truck and check on Red. She needed to pull herself together. Understanding Ty a bit more was weakening her resolve against him, and she wasn't ready for that. She thought she understood Jeff, and she ended up being a side piece that he had cast aside.

She didn't want to risk the same scenario with Ty, which was why she planned to stay firmly inside her lines and make sure Ty stayed within his.

But that didn't stop her from thinking about crossing those lines.

Ty walked her through the cold therapy process as she stood at Red's head, running her palm soothingly over Red's forehead.

With nimble fingers, Ty unwrapped the bandage around the mare's leg. To her dismay, the area was still swollen. She swallowed her concern as Ty gently prodded around the area. The way he moved and the easy confidence with which he assessed the mare made it impossible to look away. Especially after feeling his hand on hers. The heat of his touch felt branded against her skin.

Ty's entire focus was on the horse, and Red wasn't antsy as Ty moved around her feet, something the mare normally hated. A few times, Red even dropped her head to nuzzle the back of Ty's shoulder.

First her best friend, then her neighbor, and now her horse

was siding with Ty. The cards were certainly stacking against her.

With the ice pack in place, Ty straightened from the ground, hands on his hips. "We'll leave this in place for a bit, and then bandage her back up. These first few weeks will be pretty much the same. After we get the swelling down, we can ease her into a workout routine."

She let out a shaky breath. It was one thing to see her dreams for this season down the tubes. It was another to see her horse injured. What if Red never ran a barrel again? How would she ever forgive herself?

"Is she going to recover from this?"

Ty tucked his hands in his pockets. "Based on the ultrasound, it looks like a strain, and while it will take some time to recover, it isn't too severe, which is good. I think we can have her recovered and recuperated before the NFR."

"I suck at waiting," she muttered. "I really thought this was our year, and I hate that I'm upset about our year when my mare is injured."

"Be patient. And don't forget you have next year. This one accident isn't going to kill your talent." Ty shifted until he was facing her. "And Red will recover. I will do everything I can to make sure she recovers as much and as quickly as possible."

And when she looked up in his blue eyes, she found nothing but open honesty.

For the first time, she trusted him. She knew that Ty was going to do everything possible.

She worked her jaw. Suddenly she wanted to tell him more—how much she worried that she wouldn't be seen as good enough now that she couldn't race, how lonely it was on her own in that trailer, how she sometimes felt lonely even with the support of her neighbors and Jordan. The urge battered against her worn barriers.

"Ella, what's up?" Ty touched her jaw with the tip of his finger, forcing her eyes up to his face.

Something about the concern on his face forced a crack in her wall.

"I feel guilty," she whispered. "I had this dream to buy a ranchette. Something that had a little house, a barn, and enough land that I could train barrel horses."

As though he could sense her vulnerability, Ty stepped closer. Her body warmed, and she found herself leaning closer to him.

"Ella." Ty cupped her jaw in his palm. With the edge of his thumb, he slowly traced the line of her cheek. She tilted her head back, the movement complete instinct as Ty dropped his face close to hers, his eyes searching her expression.

"Yes?" she whispered.

"This will work out. You're a fighter, and so is Red. This accident wasn't your fault and being worried about your future doesn't make you a bad horse owner. You're doing everything you can for Red. She's here, with me, and I promise she'll get the best care possible."

Ty shifted until his body was inches from hers. Less than inches. Millimeters. And he still wasn't close enough.

She could see the soft little curls of hair where the top two buttons of his shirt were undone. The urge to run her hands over those curls raked through her. The scent of pine and Ty was making her weak, and she wanted to lean into him, and allow herself to be supported by him.

"Ty?"

"Hmm?" His voice was a low satin growl that sent her mind down a path it shouldn't go down, but she was helpless to stop it.

Heat bloomed low in her belly, and her gaze dropped to his lips.

Ty had gorgeous lips. Not thin, but not too full. Well-defined. Like god himself chiseled them to perfection.

When she looked up, his gaze was on her, intense, hot. His hooded eyes were drinking her in, like he was trying to memorize her.

This was the man who saved her at the dance, drove her to the hospital, insisted on taking care of her horses, and all she had done was sit on her high horse and look down at him, because of things that may not have been totally true. Things she might have decided without looking too closely at the situation.

"I'm starting to think that maybe I misjudged you." The words came out softer than she intended. Her throat felt tight, and a decade of regret came crashing down on her. "I never thanked you for everything you've done for me this past week. I've been an ass, and you've been—" *Perfect.*

"I don't need thanks," Ty said. His lips were parted, welcoming, inviting.

He was doing this for her. That was his payoff—helping her.

She licked her lips, suddenly needing him more than she

needed anything else.

And before her mind could disagree with her body, she wrapped her hand around his neck and kissed him.

CHAPTER SIX

Ty's LIPS MET Ella's, his mouth firm, unyielding.

Had she misread him?

She froze, her mouth against his. Excuses reeled through her mind as she started to pull away. Then, with a groan, he wrapped a strong arm around her waist and pulled her tight against him.

His firm lips softened against hers, and then he was claiming her, tasting her, exploring the terrain of her lips. With his free hand, he cupped the back of her head, burying his fingers in her hair.

A moan escaped her, and Ty took advantage of her parted lips to deepen the kiss, tangling his tongue with hers.

The taste of Ty melted on her tongue, driving her wild. All she could think of was more. The man kissed with such control, everything carefully restrained.

It was crazy, given their past, given who he was and she was, but she wanted him to let go and be as wild as the Montanan lands that surrounded him. As wild as he made her feel.

She arched against him, her hands going to his waistband. She needed to feel him, and she was not going to allow herself to think or analyze or do anything but feel.

The scent of outdoors surrounded them—alfalfa and horses, damp soil and the prairie heat. It blended with the leather and pine scent of Ty.

A slight breeze picked up, cooling her heated skin. She pushed herself closer against him, molding the curves of her body against his granite planes.

With a groan and a curse, he eased her back until her butt was pressed against the back of the pickup truck.

"I want you up here," he muttered. Before she could respond, he dropped the tailgate and lifted her up to sit on the edge. She spread her thighs, granting him room to fit his body between her legs, pressing her core against the growing hardness in his jeans.

Still it was not enough. She wanted him closer, naked, and next to her. Why? She wasn't going to waste time answering nagging questions when she wanted him so badly. It was like some primitive force had come alive in her.

He released her lips, grazing his mouth and teeth along her jawline. Holding him close, she tilted her head back, granting him access. Ty buried his hands in the curtain of hair, wrapping his hand in the mass until he cupped the base of her head as he continued to play with the sensitive spots along her ear and jaw.

The wind picked up, swirling around them, trapping them in a world all their own.

She nipped at his earlobe, her teeth grazing along his flesh. The bite was not nice or sweet, and Ty lost it.

Pulling her mouth back to his, the kiss grew harder, firmer, needier.

Ty's hands dropped to her ribs, bracketing her body as his thumb grazed the soft underside of her breasts.

Her breath hitched at the exploratory touch, and it was all she had to not rip her shirt off to give him access to her skin.

Heat pooled between her legs, and she wrapped her uninjured leg around his thigh, trying to pull him even closer.

She could feel his dick straining against his jeans, pressing up against her denim-clad core. The years of denial were building up to this one moment.

Ty slipped his hands under the hem of her tank. The feel of his calluses against her skin was driving her crazy. She ground her body against his, her hips undulating in a rhythm that he matched. This was all instinct, pure and simple.

His fingers were tracing intoxicating paths up and down her body, she wanted to see where they ended.

More. More. More.

Her body screamed to take this man she kept at bay for so long.

A door slammed shut, echoing across the yard, jolting her back to reality.

Ty released her so quickly, she almost fell off the edge of the tailgate. He caught her just in time.

In seconds flat, he had her shirt straightened, and his button-down tucked neatly back into his jeans.

Her face felt hot, her body was burning with desire, and her lips were beyond swollen.

And she yearned for more.

Ty's chest expanded as he tried to gather his breath.

"That must be Colton or Ty," he breathed, bracing his hands on either side of her, dropping his head so his forehead touched hers.

"Probably good timing," she said, trying to reel herself in. She pulled her hair over her shoulder and ran her fingers through the waves. She couldn't quite look at him. If she did, she'd probably jump him all over again. "That may have gone a little too far."

Ty's face instantly went blank. And just like that the cowboy teetering on the edge of losing control went back to the serious, quiet vet.

Her jaw slackened at his sudden mood change, but she quickly clamped her mouth shut.

Fine then. Two could play at this cool, calm game.

TY HAD SPENT years fantasizing about what it would be like to kiss Ella James Sanders. Years. And the real deal did not even come close to the fantasy. Too bad his brother had to step outside, interrupting them. Then again, it was probably for the best. Who knew where they would have ended up? He had been ready to take her in the bed of his truck, which was not an ideal situation.

The rest of the time at the ranch was quiet and awkward. Ella seemed to be a bit more wary around him. As though she hadn't expected the kiss to be that explosive either. She kept looking at him like she was expecting something, but what, he didn't know. And she didn't seem willing to volunteer it.

His heart hammered just thinking about that sinful kiss. The woman could easily have him wrapped around her finger, and that made him nervous. What happened if he fell for her, and she decided the leave? After the pain of Colton leaving ten years ago, and then his mother leaving shortly after that, he didn't want to handle the heartbreak of being left again. It wasn't worth the risk.

After dropping Ella off, he had headed back to work. It was a busy afternoon at the vet practice, but it kept him distracted from Ella and that kiss, so Ty chalked it up as a win. Afterward, he stopped by the feedstore to pick up some salt licks and headed home. By the time he came in the front door, Jace was making dinner for everyone.

The eldest Hartman brother had an array of cold cuts laid out and was busy making sub sandwiches. His movements were deft and sharp. Like a guy who didn't believe in doing anything in a roundabout way.

Colton wasn't anywhere in sight. This was the first time Ty had a moment to catch up with Jace since the conversation after moving the broken wheel line. Now seemed like a good time to pick it back up.

Ty dropped his boots in the mudroom before wandering to the fridge.

"Beer?" Ty pulled an unopened bottle from the fridge.

"Nah, I'm good." Jace didn't stop his movements.

"Mind if we carry on the conversation from the other day?" He grabbed some plates and napkins from the cupboard and set them down next to Jace.

"Sure," Jace said, giving Ty a wary glance. "But don't expect me to change my mind. Nothing to do with you and Colton, but I'm pretty set on heading back to Texas at this point."

"What do you plan to do with the ranch?" Ty braced his hands on the lip of the kitchen counter and squeezed. Part of him didn't want to hear the answer, even though he asked. Once Jace owned one-third of the property, he could do whatever he wanted with it.

Jace shrugged. "Sell it? I could give you guys the first offer if you would like. I know how much this ranch means to you."

But not to me.

Jace's words hung unspoken.

Ty flinched. Despite his best efforts to help his brother feel comfortable at the Rocking H, it was clear Jace didn't feel that way.

"I used to hate it here too." Ty rubbed at the back of his neck. "Beau was not a great father. He made Colton's life hell, and I didn't seem to exist in his eyes. Hell, I still feel that way. I was the one who stuck around, kept the ranch going, and made sure that we didn't lose it when Beau hit rock bottom. And yet—" Ty opened his hands, spreading his fingers "—here I am, still fighting for the ranch that I had worked so hard to keep."

He wanted to say more, but he couldn't find the magic words to get Jace to change his mind. Heavy bootsteps echoed on the porch, announcing Colton's arrival, followed by the door quickly opening and closing.

Ty glanced at Jace, who looked relieved at the interruption.

"Good, you're both here," Colton said. "I have an idea I want to bounce off you."

Colton's sudden excitement overwhelmed the room, clashing with the tension between Ty and Jace.

Colton dropped his gloves into the basket and kicked off his boots. "We should consider expanding the livestock herds. I've been looking it over, and we can easily double the cows and still manage the work between the three of us. Gus keeps finding ways to save on construction costs, and we may have enough leftover cash to buy more cows."

Colton stopped short, as though suddenly sennsing the tension in the room. The wide smile on his face faded as he looked between Ty and Jace. "What's up, guys?"

Ty looked at Jace. There was no way he was going to announce Jace's plans for him. It was on the eldest Hartman to bring it up.

Jace grimaced, as though he could read Ty's mind.

"Ty and I were talking about my return to Houston after this year is up," Jace said, his voice firm.

Colton looked to Ty to confirm, and Ty silently nodded.

"Why?" Colton pulled his hat from his head and set it upside down on the kitchen table. "Don't you like it here?"

"I don't belong here," Jace stated matter-of-factly. Like his mind was set, and he wasn't going to change it. "This isn't my legacy."

"Bull," Colton said quickly, his voice forceful. Both Jace and Ty turned to stare at him. "This land is as much yours as it is ours. If your issue is with Beau, trust me, we all have issues with him."

Jace's face went stony, his eyes gray glints of granite. "Look, you guys can buy me out if you like, but I'm not sticking around."

"What if the ranch is profitable?" Ty blurted. He cringed as he realized what he just said.

"Is the ranch profitable?" Jace asked, setting the mustard knife down.

Ty actually couldn't remember the last time the ranch was in the black. "I think we'll break even this year." Fingers crossed.

"Why would I keep a share of the ranch if it isn't profitable?" Jace asked.

"It's not profitable yet," Colton said, catching on to Ty's thinking. "We could start a breeding and training program and sell horses. However, it would be something we would need to build up to."

Ty felt a little jolt of relief that Colton wanted to start a training program. It proved that Colton planned to stick around.

If the pressure point therapy was successful with Red, there was a chance that he could expand his vet practice to the ranch. If cowboys such as Josh and Roy really did send their horses to him as part of the recovery process, the practice could be successful enough to make the ranch profitable.

If Jace kept ownership of the ranch for a few years, and the practice was profitable, Ty could probably pull enough savings together again to take out a loan to buy Jace out. That way, he could have his dream of expanding his vet practice and keep the ranch in the family.

Granted that scenario would involve a lot of debt that he hadn't planned through yet. A better scenario would be to convince Jace the ranch was worth sticking around for.

Jace went back to making the sub sandwiches, a furrow between his brows. The eldest Hartman did not look remotely convinced about Colton's idea.

Ty had to do something.

"I want to expand my vet practice to the ranch." He blurted out the words.

Jace looked up, eyebrows raised. He looked intrigued by the idea.

Emboldened by his brother's expression, Ty continued. "If this pressure point therapy with Red is successful, I could expand to the ranch. It will give me room to keep more animals, to invest time in new medicine and therapies, and to hire on more veterinarians."

"You want to expand your practice to the Rocking H?" Colton asked. He ran his hand over his chin as Ty nodded. "You've never mentioned this before. It's actually not a bad idea."

"So Red would need to recover in order for this idea to be successful?" Jace asked.

"If the horse has a successful recovery by the NFR," Ty pointed out. It was still too early to tell if Red would have a successful recovery, but Ty was willing to go out on a limb here. If they could get Jace to stop thinking about selling the place, maybe they could get him to focus on the things he did love about the ranch. It was always harder to sell something you love. "I don't have a doubt in my mind she will be recovered by then. I've been talking with a few cowboys at the rodeos, and they said if this therapy is successful, they would send their horses to me."

It was a bit of a stretch, but Jace didn't need to know what.

Ty just needed a distraction to keep Jace from considering selling the ranch and focus instead on what the ranch could be turned into. If Red was that distraction, then Ty was going to run with it.

"If Red recovers quickly," Ty continued, "it would be a great way to build up a large base of clientele and it would help us break into a sport therapy market for horses."

"And what benefit is this to the Rocking H?" Jace asked, ever savvy.

"To start, I'll have my practice lease the land. You can receive a portion of the lease. If you do me the favor of holding the land for now, I can start saving to buy you out in a few years." Ideally by then, Jace would decide he didn't want to sell.

There it was—his half-baked plan on the table.

Jace drummed his fingers against the counter, and Ty could tell his brother was thinking it over carefully.

Ty hated the fact his brother viewed this as a business transaction. It was frustrating that despite how far the three of them had come since finding out each other existed, there was still a long way to go.

And after the year was up, they may never get that chance again.

He hated that Beau did this to them.

"If you can get the horse to heal on time, prove that you can get a client list going, and that the ranch will start operating in the black, I'll hold onto my share," Jace said. "Otherwise, there's no reason why I should keep it. The cash would be a nice investment into my business."

"How much time are you willing to give us?" Ty asked. He

needed to know how much time he had to work with to expand the practice and to save up more cash.

"Let's see how the horse heals first. If she makes it to the NRF, I'm willing to talk." Jace grabbed a plate and set a sub sandwich on it before heading toward the back porch. "I'm eating outside."

"I had no idea Jace felt that way," Colton muttered as soon as Jace was out of earshot. He grabbed a sandwich and some chips before dropping down onto the kitchen stool next to Ty.

"I think he's dealing with the same issues we've been dealing with. Same father, different scars. This is how he's sorting it out. He doesn't feel like he belongs here. In a way, I don't blame him," Ty said, grabbing a plate.

His brother shook his head. "I still find it hard to believe. Jace looks happy on the ranch, and I know Hailey loves it here."

Funny to hear Colton say that when less than six months ago, his older brother wanted nothing more than to walk away from his legacy. While part of him kept expecting Colton to just up and disappear again without any notice, his brother had been going out of his way to prove how dedicated he was to the ranch.

"Jace thinks the legacy is ours and not his," he added.

"Because our terrible father abandoned him?" Colton asked.

"I guess he doesn't realize what a blessing it was," Ty added drily.

Colton grabbed the bag of chips and munched on them thoughtfully. "I can't afford to buy him out. Not when I'm trying to start this new company branch. We could pool our cash together and buy him out now."

"That kills my plan to expand the vet practice. I've been saving for this for years," Ty said, studying his knuckles. It was the first time he came close to admitting how much he wanted this dream.

"I'd hate to take that off the plate then," Colton said without hesitation. "The best we can do is try to make this ranch profitable as quickly as possible, and then buy him out as soon as we can."

Ty pressed the tips of his fingers together. "Let's think about this for a bit. Hailey loves it here, and the more Jace is tied to the land, the harder it will be for him to leave. If we can come up with a way to make the ranch more profitable, great. However, if we can convince Jace to keep his share, that would be ideal."

Because Ty really did want his brother to stay. He liked having his family in one spot. It made life at the ranch richer. And whether Jace saw it or not, he was one of the Hartman brothers.

Colton tapped his fingers on the countertop.

"We can wait and see if Red makes a full recovery," Colton said after a minute. "But I think we should also be proactive. One thing we know about Jace is that he likes to build things from the ground up. There's nothing on the ranch that wasn't here before him."

Normally it grated on Ty when Colton tried to take charge. It drove him nuts his brother disappeared for ten years and then came back expecting everyone to follow his lead when Ty was the one who held the ranch together. However, this time he knew Colton was onto something.

"We need to get Jace onto something that is new and that he can create from scratch," Ty said, his mind already running through possible ideas.

"Exactly," Colton agreed. "Let's spend some time thinking about it and see what we can come up with. We have seven months to change Jace's mind. Let's figure something out."

THE STUBBORN COWBOY was back the following morning, tossing hay into Mickey's feeder like nothing had happened. As though he hadn't kissed her senseless yesterday.

That kiss had been on replay in her head. Her eyes felt swollen from lack of sleep, but every time she closed her eyes, the feel of his hands sliding across her body came racing back, and it left her wanting more.

There was no way she'd let herself have more. Not now, when everything was up in the air with her career. Everything was good while she was the top barrel racer in the state, but what happened if Red didn't recover and she was back to being Ella James Sanders, the girl from the wrong end of town?

Part of her hoped that the awkwardness after their kiss would be reason enough for him to stop showing up.

Apparently, Ty always followed through, no matter the circumstance.

"Morning," he called out, his voice perfectly normal.

A car drove by, gave a honk and the person inside waved.

She didn't recognize who it was, but Ty must have because he waved back.

She kept her hands firmly on her crutch grips.

"Morning," she tried, but her throat felt tight, and the word came out more as a croak. Ty looked amazing this morning. Dark Wranglers, a light blue button-up, and a straw hat. No doubt that blue shirt did incredible things to his eyes, and there was no way she was foolish enough to get close enough to confirm. Just having him here was doing funny little things low in her belly. She was determined to ignore it, and to not complicate her life further when it was already a mess.

Even if every time Ty tossed a flake of hay, his muscles flexed to perfection.

Mickey let out a high-pitched whinny, breaking Ella from her thoughts.

Her mare was ignoring the hay. Instead, she pressed against the fence, her neck stretched high, sniffing at the air.

A smaller, higher whinny came back in response.

What the—?

She'd been so busy looking at Ty, she hadn't even looked at his truck.

Or noticed the tiny two-horse trailer behind it.

A trailer that shifted as the animal inside once again whinnied back.

"Is there a horse in that trailer?" she asked, suddenly curious as she headed down the crooked porch steps. Her movements had become more fluid after a week on the crutches.

"It's a pony." Ty wasn't smiling, but there was a softness in his eyes that she'd never noticed before. Or maybe she'd never wanted to notice. Who could say?

Quickly she looked away.

Ty appeared undeterred. He ambled over, thumbs in his front pockets, and stopped a few feet away, legs planted in the ground. "You left your door open."

Crinkling her nose, she looked up. "Excuse me?"

He pointed at the door. "Your door is open. You always leave it shut."

Biting her lip, she stared at the door. Sure enough, she had left it open, granting a view of the worn brown carpet and tiny ancient kitchen. Letting him see where she actually lived was like giving him a glimpse of her life and into things she wanted to hide, or change.

Mickey called again, still not interested in her breakfast when there was a new friend to be made. The mare's strong dark body glistened in the morning light as she paced back and forth.

"So did you bring the pony here to torture my lonely horse?" she asked, turning back to him. His hat was pulled low so that she couldn't see his eyes. Only the firm cut of those full lips that she had kissed yesterday.

And wanted to kiss again.

Damn it.

"The Millers are retiring and selling their herds. All the horses have been sold; however, they still have this pony they had bought for their grandchildren," Ty explained.

She nodded slowly. "And you have the pony because?"

Ty shrugged. "I told them you had a lonely mare, and I offered to take the pony off their hands."

"Whoa, whoa, whoa." She held up her hands, clutching the crutches close with her elbows. "I don't need any favors. From you or the Millers."

"Hey, I'm just helping out two lonely herd animals. I don't like the habits Mickey is picking up," Ty said. His calm voice held an air of authority, like he was in vet mode.

She was not going to be fooled by vet mode.

Mickey let out another shrill greeting.

"I can't afford one more mouth to feed, and we can't just put the pony in with Mickey. We don't know if they'll get along."

"I've solved that problem already," Ty called over his shoulder, heading to the trailer as though she hadn't turned down the pony. "And I brought you breakfast."

He nodded toward the foil-wrapped package on the hood of the truck.

Her traitorous stomach growled. "Colton cooked again?"

"I did. Pancakes and bacon. Hope that works for you." Ty handed the warm foil package over to her. It smelled sweet and savory.

Her mouth watered. "You trying to butter me up?"

"If it makes it so you don't freak out and reject the pony, then yes, I'm trying to butter you up."

Ty headed to the trailer and opened one door. The pony did not appear. Instead, Ty pulled out some green fence panels.

"You brought a fence?" Did this guy think of everything?

She tried to ignore the little blooms of heat that were bubbling through her body as he went about setting up six panels into a little enclosure.

"Just until these two get used to each other," he explained.

"I haven't agreed to the pony," she reminded him. She opened the foil packet, slipped a piece of bacon out, and bit into it. Oh god. It was amazing. Crispy, meaty, salty.

"You haven't seen Maverick yet," Ty said, his voice echoing in the tiny metal trailer. Seconds later, small hooves hit the packed gravel driveway, clopping daintily.

The 'hello' the tiny silver Shetland pony screeched was not at all small, though.

"Ms. Minna is going to kill me," she muttered. Closing her eyes, she popped the last bit of bacon into her mouth. Damn the man was good. The plan to butter her up was working.

Ty led the pony into the makeshift pen where Maverick and Mickey were close enough that they could check each other out, but not close enough that they could cause damage if they didn't like each other.

Mickey looked thrilled. She paced back and forth, pausing to check out the tiny pony across the fence. Maverick ducked his head before reaching out his delicate nose to greet Mickey in return.

Damn it. The vet did good.

Somehow, he managed to help both of her horses.

And her.

A warm thrill rushed through her.

"The Millers don't mind?" she asked reluctantly.

He shook his head. "I told them I would buy him if no seller came up. I can't imagine he'll be available for much longer. He's a pretty sweet little guy. A good 4-H pony."

The pony was cute, and he didn't take up too much room.

"I'll give him a one-week trial," she finally relented.

"The Millers will give him to you at a discount—"

She held up her hands, stopping him. "I don't need a discount." She was capable of paying for her animals—even if it did take a little more out of her savings.

Ty shot her an exasperated look. "It was a friends discount, not a sympathy discount."

"Right," she dragged out, but she let it drop and went for a change in subject. "Thanks for the breakfast."

Ty motioned toward the small stack of hay. She followed, grateful to get off her crutches, and sat down next to him, the sweet scent of hay blurring with Ty's leather and pine scent.

He shifted on the hay bale until there was only an inch gap between his jean-clad leg and her bare one.

The foil packet containing her breakfast felt warm and heavy in her hand. Or maybe it was her whole body that felt warm and heavy. She wanted to lean into him, sink her weight against him, and, yes, damn it, kiss him.

Ty's phone buzzed, breaking into her thoughts before her mind traveled too far down the wrong dirt road.

Ty scanned the name on the screen, hit the red X to ignore the call, and dropped his hands between his knees, clasping the device between his palms.

Ella felt the back of her neck grow warm. "You can't ignore Mom. If you want privacy, I can head into the house—"

"Mom left me at seventeen to move to Idaho to marry some guy. I'm okay ignoring her." Ty leaned back, bracing his body against the stack of hay behind them, not quite looking at her.

Ella turned to stare at him. "Your mom left you? I thought you stuck around to finish high school." She dropped her gaze back to her hands. "Although, I guess that's what I heard. I never actually asked you."

Was this the second story about Ty she had misinterpreted? She shifted on the hay. Maybe she should have given Ty more credit back then.

"I did decide to stay here. It's my home. My heritage is here. My legacy. I thought if I stayed, she'd—" He broke off, pulling his hat even lower.

"But she didn't stay." Ella pulled a small piece of buttery pancake from the foil and chewed thoughtfully. "When was the last time you saw her?"

"We hadn't talked in years, but after Dad's funeral, she started calling again. She tried calling the first couple years after she left, but I was so angry, I never answered."

"So that's why you moved to the ranch your senior year?" she said, recalling how withdrawn Ty had become during school—the usually outgoing teen had seemed sullen those first few months of the school year. Even she'd noticed.

"She left town so fast to marry this dude, it was a blur. She dropped me at the Rocking H and didn't look back."

She couldn't imagine not talking to her parents for years. Despite the fact her parents had moved to Oregon two years ago, she still spoke with them weekly. She liked to hear the happiness in her dad's voice as he talked about the hardware store he was managing, and the calm in her mom's voice after a day of working in her bookstore. They'd both had a chance to start over, and it had really changed them.

Like Ty, she had chosen to stay. Despite never measuring up for some people, there were things about the place that she couldn't imagine leaving—her neighbors, her roots, the life she planned for herself. Yes, she had things to prove to those people, and frankly, she was enjoying doing just that. Her father had felt his wrong-side-of-the-tracks legacy strongly, and he'd needed a new locale to find his true self, but Ella…she could prove her worth right here. Lindsey and Jeff and all the snobs could bite it.

"Maybe she wants to reconcile," she tried.

"I'm not sure if I'm ready." Ty leaned forward and rested his elbows on his knees, and opened his hands, palms up. The tips of his fingers touched, and she found herself staring at the hands that less than twenty-four hours ago were clamped around her waist and creating a delicious friction that still left traces of desire burning low in her belly.

Suddenly her heart ached for the younger, teenaged Ty. The guy she'd thought who had it all—popularity, horses, money, confidence. Turned out he was struggling as well. His struggle was very much different from hers, but it was a struggle nonetheless.

Unsure of what to do, but still wanting to provide comfort, she twisted on the bale, the bits of hay poking into the backs of her legs where her black shorts exposed her bare legs. Quietly, she placed her hand on his shoulder.

Even through his tee, she could feel the warmth of his skin. Some crazy part of her wanted to slip her fingers under the sleeve.

Ty let out a soft laugh. "I'm not even sure why I'm sharing

this with you."

Ella shrugged. "Maybe you trust me?"

He snorted. "Ironic considering you don't trust me."

She pushed his hat back, revealing those bright blue eyes that put the Montana sky to shame. The blue shirt did offset them to perfection. "Thanks for bringing the pony. I'm sure Mickey will love having a friend."

One corner of his mouth crooked up wryly. "I know what it's like to be alone. I'd hate for any of the creatures in my care to feel lonely as well."

He ran the pad of his thumb softly along her jawline. Just that single, simple touch was enough to spark warmth flooding through her body, hurtling to her core, heating her skin at his touch.

She was sinking fast, and her resolve was melting away as quickly as ice on a summer day.

Clearing his throat, Ty climbed to his feet. "May as well finish up. I can drive you out to see Red."

Just like that, Ty made it clear that he wasn't interested in more.

She prayed that her face didn't show her disappointment as she watched the cowboy walk away.

However, she knew now why his barriers were up. He was protecting himself.

Despite what he said, he didn't trust her. And the reality of that truth stung to her core.

CHAPTER SEVEN

"WHAT ARE WE doing here?" Ella asked as Ty pulled his truck into the parking lot in front of Joe's Deli.

It had been three days since Ty brought the pony over, and, as much as she hated to admit it, he was right. Mickey was much happier with some equine company and had stopped cribbing and pawing. She'd decided to put the two together tomorrow, and Ty agreed to the plan. Considering Mickey was constantly standing near the pony's enclosure, trying to be closer, Ella had a feeling the transition would be smooth.

"Getting lunch. On me," Ty said turning off the truck. "Unless you're happy with whatever you packed in that paper bag."

She glanced down at the brown paper bag at her feet that contained yet another peanut butter and jelly sandwich with some celery sticks.

Not exactly the lunch of champions. After she bought her ranch and got it running, she would be happy to never see another PB and J again. However, at the moment, she had bread and peanut butter in the pantry, and she was grateful for that.

"I'm good."

Ty turned to her. "Are you? Because this is the third time

I've picked you up around lunch, and each time you've brought the same sad sandwich in a brown paper bag."

"Wow, judge much?" She nudged the bag with her toe. "What if I happen to like my lunches?" After all, that sandwich was *her* sad sandwich.

Ty held up his hands. "Fine. But now I'm wondering, how are you doing on groceries?"

She narrowed her eyes. Her supplies were running low, but if she became desperate, she could go with Ms. Minna on her grocery social outing. She wasn't that desperate yet. She still had eggs, peanut butter, bread, and part of a casserole.

"I'm fine."

A muscle ticked in Ty's jaw as he studied her, as though trying to read her mind. "It wouldn't hurt to accept help sometimes."

Accept help? She accepted plenty of help—from Jordan and her two neighbors. She was just about to tell him so when he opened the door and got out of the truck.

Pushing open her door, she scrambled out, struggling with her crutches. "I accept help."

"Yeah, after it's forced on you," Ty retorted over his shoulder.

Ty opened the worn wood door and waited until she caught up, holding it open for her.

To prove her point, she swallowed the comment that she could hold the door herself and headed inside.

Joe's Deli hadn't changed since Joe started the place decades ago. He had since retired, and his son Mike now ran the place. Mike's kids were frequently helping out, and one smiled at her as they approached the counter.

Rock music from the late fifties and early sixties played overhead as she breathed in the scent of sweet ice cream and fresh-baked bread. She inhaled deeply, her argument with Ty ebbing from her mind. Going to Joe's was a treat for her. Something that she did on occasion when she wanted something special for lunch.

Coming in on a random Tuesday was not special. She quickly calculated how this would affect her weekly budget, which was already stretched tight as Ty cared for Red. Hopefully, Ty's therapy was working, and she'd be back on the rodeo circuit before she knew it and earning her big paycheck once more.

It was just before noon, so she and Ty were the only customers at the moment. Thank god. Between Ms. Minna and the rumor mill, there was enough gossip rolling around about the two of them without adding fuel to the fire by getting lunch together.

"You ready to order?" Ty asked. His expression was sharp, assessing, as though he were daring her to not accept his offer.

"I can accept help," she hissed at him. "Ordering lunch isn't going to prove that."

Ty gave a lazy shrug. "Sure. I see you do it all the time."

She chose to ignore the thin veneer of sarcasm.

Ty continued, "I'm just saying that maybe you should give the people of this town the benefit of the doubt. It's not like they're out to get you."

No, but judging how they talked about her father who almost lost their home after they sold the horses and the feedstore closed, the people of this town weren't exactly supportive either.

Head held high, just to show Ty she could accept an offer, she ordered an Italian sub.

She'd save her PB and J for dinner tonight.

Ty moved next to her to place his order. He wasn't touching her, but his nearness made her all too aware of him. That kiss was still at the forefront of her mind, and despite the fact they hadn't kissed since, her body seemed to be in tune to his every move. Ty's scent wrapped around her like a warm hug.

Since the conversation about his mom, the man kept his distance, but she frequently caught him looking at her with heat in his eyes.

It was thrilling and unnerving at the same time. It didn't help she kept noticing little details about him, like the freckles on his cheeks that were impossible to see unless you were up close. Every time she noticed something new, she found herself wondering, just how wrong was she about Ty?

Maybe her grudge against him was as misplaced as her father's grudge against the entire Hartman clan. She still hadn't told her father about Red staying at the Rocking H, though she had mentioned her horse was getting therapy. Eventually she'd have to say something.

She gripped her crutches tighter and eased herself from the space. Pulling her wallet out of her pocket, she handed Ty a ten, which he waved away.

"Take it," she insisted, and tucked the bill into the front pocket of his shirt.

Her fingers brushed the hard plane on his chest. It was an

innocent, unconscious move, but a warm spark raced from the tips of her fingers to deep in her core.

She swallowed, her fingers still pressed against his hard muscle, feeling the heat of his body against the sensitive pads of her hand.

What would it be like to touch him without his shirt?

She glanced up at him.

His face was stony. The only hint that he felt anything was the color staining his high cheekbones.

The cafe door opened, and a blond woman stepped in.

Sucking in a sharp breath, Ella dropped her hand and turned away. Of all the people to walk in, Lindsey was the last person she wanted to see. She wasn't ready to face the other woman, not after the accident. She didn't want to hear the gloat or smugness in Lindsey's voice.

Holding perfectly still, Ella did her best to blend with the old-school fifties' décor of the sandwich shop, thought it was probably next to impossible as she stood next to a six-foot-something vet. Ty, who was wrapping up the order, hadn't even noticed Lindsey.

Maybe it wasn't too late to run to the bathroom. If Lindsey was focused on Ty—

"Ella." Lindsey's voice rang out across the shop.

Damn it. Ella's shoulders crept up to her ears.

"I'm surprised to see you here." The smile on Lindsey's face didn't quite reach her eyes as the other woman took in the crutches Ella had tucked tightly against her sides.

As usual, Lindsey was decked to the nines—her expensive chandelier earrings caught the sunlight filtering through the window, her sheer black top offset her pale hair, and no doubt there were rhinestones on the back pockets of what looked like brand-new designer jeans.

Ella wished she could pull her arm across her stomach and cover the plain black tank she had pulled on over her worn, cutoff shorts. Her white sneakers, while new, were nowhere near as fancy as the strappy leather sandals Lindsey had on her manicured feet.

"Congrats on placing first in Dillon's rodeo. It wasn't my best run that weekend, but—" Lindsey's eyes dropped pointedly to the crutches. "I guess that doesn't matter anyway. How long are you out for?"

Gritting her teeth, Ella forced herself to ignore the barb. Pushing her shoulders back, she swallowed the retort on her tongue. Lindsey did not have a good run this past weekend, and Ella was still leading in the standings.

"Long enough," Ella said, keeping it vague.

"Shame." Lindsey's gaze moved behind Ella, and the smile on her face grew. "Hey there, cowboy."

Ella rolled her eyes.

"Lindsey. Didn't expect to see you here," Ty said easily.

The warmth in his voice irritated Ella.

"Just grabbing some lunch." Lindsey looked between the two of them, interest sparking in her eyes. "So, are the rumors true?"

Ella didn't dare look at Ty. The last time she confessed feelings for Ty to Lindsey, she ended up being a victim of a high school prank. Granted they were older and wiser, but she wasn't willing to put herself out there again.

While Ella knew that Lindsey and Ty still hung out on occasion, the blatant interest on the other woman's face did not sit well.

"Italian sandwich and turkey club," the high school kid behind the counter called.

Thank god. Despite being on crutches, she managed to beat Ty to the counter. At least the kid had the foresight to put everything in a plastic bag, making it easier to carry.

Grabbing their lunch, she turned in time to see Lindsey tilt her head as she peered up at Ty. Her long curls spilled flirtatiously past her shoulder and over her breast.

"Maybe we can hang out sometime. It's been a while," the blond woman said.

Ella's gut tightened and she squeezed the plastic handles of the bag.

She was not jealous. She was *not* jealous.

Okay, maybe just a little. But she was also tired of Lindsey always getting what she wanted.

"We should get going," Ella said, her voice brusque. Ty looked at her like she just dropped in from another planet, but he didn't argue with her.

"Call me," Lindsey called after them. "Feel better soon."

The last words felt like an afterthought, and Ella was surprised Lindsey didn't add "but not too soon." After all, the longer Ella was out, the better chance Lindsey had to qualify for the NFR.

One thing was for certain, she didn't want Lindsey to qualify. The sooner she and Red recovered, the better. She needed back in the game as quickly as possible.

AFTER LEAVING JOE'S Deli, Ella morphed from a feisty cowgirl to a woman he barely knew. She stewed in the passenger seat, arms crossed as he headed to the ranch. Anxiety rolled off her in waves, and it made the roomy truck cab feel claustrophobic.

"When's the earliest Red will recover?" Her voice sounded brittle.

He slowed his rig as he approached the road that led to the Rocking H. Honestly, he didn't know if he was relieved she was finally talking or annoyed the nice lunch he had planned in his head for them was getting ruined.

Annoyed. But not because his plans were ruined.

"You're silent the entire trip back to the ranch, and the first question you ask has to do with Red's timeline? As we discussed, if the therapy goes according to plan, we said eight to ten weeks," he reminded her, trying to keep the irritation from his voice. "But it's still up in the air."

At the moment, while Red was showing improvement, it wasn't as quick as he would like.

"Fine. Whatever it takes for Red to heal as quickly as possible so I can get back out there." Her shoulders were tense, and she wasn't looking at him.

This had something to do with Lindsey. The second the other woman walked into Joe's Ella's mood turned.

Granted Lindsey wasn't the easiest person in high school. He'd heard Ella and Lindsey had a falling out their junior year though he didn't know what caused it. He always assumed it was because Lindsey had everything handed to her with minimal effort, and Ella had to earn everything in her name.

However, Lindsey had changed over the years. Life got handed to her a few times, and her breakup with Jeff seemed to open her eyes that she wasn't the most important person in the world. She was definitely working on being more empathetic with people less fortunate than her.

"I feel like there is more going on than what you're sharing with me right now," he said, keeping his voice mellow.

Ella looked out the window and didn't say anything.

Alright, fine. He had a solution to her stubborn silence.

As they reached the ranch, he didn't slow to park at the barn. Instead, he drove past the structure, past the pen where Red was kept, and toward the pasture they kept their cows during the winter.

The dirt road to the small creek was well worn over the years. The truck bumped and rolled along the path until they reached a small grove of trees.

Out of the corner of his eye, he caught Ella shooting him a questioning look, but she didn't say anything.

That's fine, he could be patient. He was a vet after all and was used to dealing with stubborn and angry animals. Patient was his middle name.

He parked by the small grove, locating the truck bed in the shade dappled with sunlight. The silence was broken by the sound of the babbling creek and the occasional lull from the cow herd nearby. In the distance, he could see the old cow dog ambling out to greet them.

This was his own peaceful paradise, quiet and private. Growing up, it was where he escaped when his father was too distant, when the absence of his family hurt too much, or when life wasn't going his way. This spot was his haven.

Hopefully, Ella, in all her prickliness, could let her spikes down for a minute to enjoy this peace. It was a small gift he was offering her.

"I thought we could enjoy lunch before working on Red," he explained as he killed the engine. The other vet at the practice was taking the afternoon appointments, so unless an emergency popped up, Ty could enjoy a longer lunch. "Do you have other plans today?"

Ella shook her head then got out of the truck. "No plans."

She looked around as he pulled the tailgate down and grabbed a woven blanket out of the emergency bag he kept in his truck in case he broke down in the middle of nowhere.

"It's beautiful out here," she added as he spread the blanket on the tailgate and set their lunch to one side.

He turned to her. "I'll help you onto the tailgate."

Her eyes went wide, and the guarded mask she wore dropped. Her face flushed, and he could see exactly where her mind was going—to that kiss only days before. He had hauled her onto the tailgate during that moment, desperate to have her wrapped around him.

His body hardened at the memory.

"Help me how?" Ella asked, her voice wary as he took the crutches from her hands and propped them on the side of the truck.

"Like this." Ty moved closer, aligning his body with hers. Her gaze followed his, and as he dropped his chin down, she tilted her head back. Her movement was miniscule, a mere fraction, but it was just enough to align her mouth with his.

All he had to do was lean down and claim her.

"I'm going to touch you," he murmured, giving her full warning so she could stop him if she wanted to.

Her pupils dilated, flooding out the green of her eyes, as she nodded.

His heart hammered in his chest, and the dry Montana air somehow felt even drier.

Bracing his legs on either side of her, he circled his hands around her waist. The warmth of her body seeped through her clothes, and he wanted nothing more than to slip his hands under her shirt and feel her soft skin.

Ella bit her lip, drawing his attention to her full mouth, and he nearly groaned.

His dick pressed hard against his zipper, and he hoped she didn't notice.

He tightened his hands around her waist and lifted her easily onto the tailgate. Her gaze never left his.

Clearing his throat, he stepped away before he did something stupid, like kiss her again.

He eased himself into the spot next to her. Grabbing the sandwiches, he pulled out both paper-wrapped packages and handed the one marked Italian over to her. "Here."

Her fingers brushed the back of his hand as she took the sandwich from him.

"Thanks." Her voice was husky, and he could see the hint of haze in her eyes.

"I like it out here," she added after a moment.

"It used to be my escape growing up. My private sanctuary.

I thought you'd like it."

Her green eyes held his, the look in them soft and under-standing, as though she knew what this place really meant to him. "Thanks for bringing me."

Ella carefully unwrapped the white paper and took a bite of her sandwich. They ate in silence as Ty tried to figure out just what to say. Unfortunately, the right words weren't coming to him. Easy and eloquent words were never his thing. So he opted to just put it out there.

"What's up with Lindsey?"

Ella went eerily still. Apparently, the blunt approach was not the best approach.

"What do you mean?" she asked.

She wasn't looking at him, her eyes focused on the food in her hand. Her thumb ran along a ridge at the top of her roll.

"Don't think I didn't notice. The second she walked into the deli, you got weird. Defensive, even."

Ella shifted in her spot, as though uncomfortable.

"We just don't get along." Her words were firm, as though she were stating a fact.

"I know you two were once friends," he tried again.

She snorted. "Sure, once I started rising in the ranks at high school rodeo, Lindsey thought it would be okay to be friends. Then when I became better than her, winning at the rodeos she used to win, she no longer saw me as a friend and more as competition. Then I made the horrid mistake of liking the same guy she did."

She looked like she was bracing herself, steeling herself for any attack from him.

"I'm sorry," he started. "I didn't know—"

Ella gave a short, bitter laugh. "Yeah, right, you didn't know."

What did that mean?

He turned toward her, but Ella was already looking away.

"Excuse me? What exactly are you implying here?" There was no way she thought he was involved in her falling out with Lindsey.

Ella scoffed. "It's nothing. Old history. We've both moved on. It's just made me wary of people, that's all."

She picked at the crust of the roll, tearing it away in chunks.

He covered her hand with his before she could mutilate the bread further.

"I'm still not clear what you're talking about. Maybe you should get it out in the open."

She shook her head.

"Ella?" he prodded.

She dropped her chin to her chest. "Why are you making me relive this?"

"I'm curious what I'm making you relive." Something wasn't adding up. What did he do that she considered so terrible? "Why don't you explain it to me?"

Ella bit her lip and then let out a breath. "Fine. It's about that prank? For prom? How you asked me to prom with the plan to ditch me that night?"

All he could do was stare. Ella shoulders hunched forward as he searched his memory for any prom prank he could recall.

None came to mind. The only event that popped up was

the time she coldly and brutally cut him down in front of everyone on the football field.

"I'm sorry, what prank?"

Her jaw dropped, and she whirled on him, her green eyes hard. "Don't play dumb with me. That stupid prank. I overheard Lindsey telling the plan to some of her friends. She was going to have one of the most popular guys in school ask me to prom and then ditch me the night of so they could laugh in my face. She knew I had a crush on you. It was the perfect revenge for someone who was clearly jealous of my success."

And just like that, the reason she rejected him so cruelly clicked into place.

He must have looked like a trout fresh out of water as he gaped at her. How on earth could she think that about him?

His brain rushed to gather his thoughts, to make sense of what she just said, but the rational side of him was giving way to a simmer of emotions he had repressed long ago.

As the silence continued, the hardness on Ella's face faded to confusion, as though she realized something wasn't quite right.

"That's why you told me you would rather take your dog to prom than some dirty cowboy?" There was a hardness to his tone that he couldn't hide, and every muscle in his body began to clench.

Her warm hand was still interlaced with his, and he released it like it was a snake he grabbed inadvertently.

Hurt and confusion ran across her features, and she crossed her arms tight over her chest.

An hour ago, he would have pulled her close. Now? There

was no way in hell.

"I… Yes. I know it was terrible, but I was trying to protect myself."

The fact she thought he could do something so cruel cut him to the quick.

"You were protecting yourself from someone who didn't what to hurt you," he snapped. "I didn't set you up. I was truly asking you to prom."

She blinked. "Excuse me?"

"I wasn't part of the prank. You're accusing me of something I didn't even know about." Just saying it out loud pissed him off even more.

Ella shook her head. "What about you and Jeff? You two always hung out; he clearly knew about the prank. I had assumed…I mean, I thought…" Her voice faded as though she put two and two together.

Ty would bet his ranch that Jeff was the guy who was supposed to ask her. It was around that time that Ty started noticing that Jeff had a mean streak he didn't like.

"Yeah, Jeff and I hung out, and yes, he turned into an awful person. That's why I ended the friendship. I didn't want to be around someone like him anymore. I had better people to spend my time with." Ty pulled at the ends of his hair. "But what on earth did I do to deserve this reputation you have of me?"

Ella seemed to be folding in on herself, her green eyes wide and overwhelmed. He didn't care. She brought this on herself.

"I had a crush on you, for years. That's why I asked you to prom." It was she who had pulled the stopper on his emotions, unbottling years of pent-up frustration. He was so tired of her thinking he was this awful person when he never deserved it. "I get that you were hurt, but that cut you gave me on the field hurt as well. You've assumed I'm some horrible person for years all because of some high school grudge."

If Ella could physically backpedal, it looked like she would have. "I—I didn't know. I just assumed—"

"If you think I'm that terrible, then why are you letting me help you out in the first place? Are you using me?" The words grated as he said them. He thought back to all the times they interacted, trying to pinpoint a moment where she could develop this perception of him.

"I'm not using you," she said, suddenly defensive. "You kept inserting yourself into the situation."

She may as well have slapped him.

Any retort he had flew out of his mind as he stared at her.

Ella tried to reach for his hand, but he pulled it away. "Ty, I'm sorry. I shouldn't—"

"How much longer are you on the crutches?" His words were flat, brittle. The same tone he used with Colton when his brother finally returned to Montana. If he spoke like he didn't care, then he couldn't care, right?

Liar.

She hesitated, clearly trying to figure out the direction he was going. "The doctor says another week, and then I can stop using them."

"Great." He rolled his sandwich up in its paper and stuffed it back in the plastic sack. He was done. He couldn't do this anymore. He wasn't going to play martyr to someone he had a crush on for over a decade and who thought he was an awful person. "I'll help you out for one more week. After that, you're on your own. I'm done trying."

Chapter Eight

S HE MESSED UP. Holy cow, did she mess up.

Ella never thought the words "I'm done" could tear through her, leaving her wounded with ripped and tattered edges. But when Ty uttered those words, hurt and anger and spite cutting across his face as he did, she felt like she was being torn apart.

The rest of the visit had been awkward, and she'd been grateful that Ty was suddenly called on an emergency visit that stopped the session short.

Ty came by the next day, barely acknowledging her with an imperceptible nod and nothing else, as he fed her horse and pony. She didn't know what this meant for Red's future therapy, but more importantly, she didn't know what this meant for her and Ty.

Now that the situation was blown wide open, and she realized that Ty was never involved, she felt foolish she had even believed that he could be. Ironic because the whole reason she even held the grudge was to prevent herself from appearing foolish in the first place. She'd been so sick of people looking at her like she was less than, that she had taken the opportunity to have a toehold above someone. And the person she picked didn't deserve her wrath one bit.

She needed to figure out a way to fix the situation. At the very least, she needed to apologize to Ty. He had to know how awful she felt, even if he never did forgive her.

She had told Ty to go ahead with Red's therapy the next couple days without her. There was no way she could handle the twenty-minute drive to his place and back. Not with the stunted conversation and the dark tension between them.

The trip back to her place after the blowup was bad enough. He didn't look at her, didn't talk to her. Just drove her to her place, dropped her off, waited until she was inside and drove off.

At least she knew that he would take care of Red in the best possible way. Leave it to her to realize that she did trust the straightforward vet once he wanted nothing to do with her.

Ella opened her cupboard and sighed as she looked at the meager offerings. The only things left were the jar of peanut butter, the end pieces of bread, and some tea.

Ty had previously mentioned groceries to her, but she couldn't call him up and ask him for help after everything that went down. Jordan would be back in another four days, but there wasn't enough food to hold her over. Which meant asking Ms. Minna or finding someone else.

Her knee twinged in complaint as she thought of Ms. Minna's endless shopping trips. Maybe there was someone else she could consider.

Ty had accused her of not being able to accept help, and maybe he had a point. After all, she was part of this community, right? Someone had to be willing to help her.

Grabbing her phone, she started scrolling through her

numbers. Quite a few of them were ones she had added after she started winning and more people approached her at bars, in public, at her job.

Maybe it was because she hadn't seemed as guarded once she saw herself as a winner.

She stopped on Gus Jones's number. She and Gus had known each other a long time. They weren't best friends, but they were close enough. She liked Gus with her grit and construction boots. Sure, she was dating Colton Hartman, but Colton seemed like a decent guy. And from what she could tell, the cowboy certainly made Gus happy.

Gus would be a good first step.

Taking a breath, Ella hit the number and waited for it to ring.

To her surprise, Gus picked up immediately.

"Ella?"

Ella straightened and cleared her throat. "Gus? Uh—hi. I'm sure it's strange I'm calling out of the blue…"

"Oh, not at all," Gus sang into the phone, and she sounded like she truly meant it. "What's up?"

"I—" Ella closed her eyes and sucked in a breath. It was now or never. "I was wondering if you could do me a favor?"

Gus laughed. "I live to help people. Of course. Tell me what it is."

Ella sagged against her kitchen counter in relief, releasing the breath from her lungs. Despite the fact her life felt like it was in utter turmoil, she found herself smiling as she made her request.

Maybe Ty had a point.

ELLA HAD BEEN giving him space over the past three days.

Part of Ty—the angry part—was relieved. He didn't want her around. He didn't want to deal with a woman who had such a low opinion of him while he helped her out and worked on her horse.

The other part of him—the part that had been attracted to her for so long—wondered if she was doing okay. It was that part of him he wanted to bury down deep. This attraction had lasted way too long. It was time to move on.

He did feel for Ella being the butt of Lindsey's prank. It was horrible, and if he had known about it at the time, he would have said something. However, Ella was so determined to not appear as less than that she ended up hiding herself away and looking down on others. And he wanted no part of it.

The day had been a busy one. He had a full plate of animal patients that didn't stop until he closed his office doors an hour later than usual. Afterward, he stopped off at Ella's to feed her horse and pony. Thankfully, she didn't come out when he dropped by. It felt like a knife to the chest to even look at her right now. Then when he got home, Colton came into the house looking grim with the report that the electric fence at the steer enclosure was down.

Jace was hidden away in the office, no doubt researching studs. He and Colton had decided that Jace could do the research for a new stud horse to purchase. Ty and Colton had given their brother some recommended requirements, a budget, and some bloodlines they were looking for, and then let Jace at it. Jace had taken the task reluctantly. At first it was clear that their brother wasn't thrilled with the idea. The fact that he knew so little about horses probably didn't sit well with Jace.

However, Ty knew they would guide Jace in the right direction in the end.

What they hadn't expected was that Jace ended up taking the task very seriously, spending hours researching bloodlines and studs for sale. Which was why when they saw the closed office door, Colton and Ty headed out to fix the fence themselves.

"Alright," he called to Colton as they finished repairing the smooth wire. "We can turn the juice back on."

Colton nodded, and they trudged back to the house together, their strides in sync.

Jace met them halfway to the house. His movements were beginning to mirror the head-down, address-the-issues-as-they-come approach that both Ty and Colton had learned from growing up on the Rocking H.

Ty smiled to himself. Despite Jace thinking he didn't belong on the ranch, it was quite clear the ranch was having its effect on Jace. It fit Jace better than he realized.

"The neighbor kid called. He asked if we wanted him and his brothers to help cut and bale hay again," Jace said as he fell in line as they headed inside.

"Great," Ty said. "Works for me."

"Me too," Colton added. "Do you want to call them back and let them know?"

Jace nodded as he pulled gloves from his back pocket and tossed them into the basket on the counter by the front door.

Ty smiled at Hailey who was sitting at the kitchen table with her laptop open, her cell phone by her side. Next to her was a small stack of papers and a notebook.

As Ty moved farther into the kitchen, he noticed the stack of papers were horses.

He pulled the top page off and studied it. To his surprise, the gorgeous sorrel stud had impressive bloodlines. In the photos, he had a strong build, a good head, and a nice line in his back. The price was a little high, but Jace was certainly going in the right direction.

"Hey," Jace came over and pulled the stack out of his hand. "I'm still researching."

The notebook and the pile of horses for sale disappeared from the table as Jace squirreled them away to the office.

Hailey smiled up at Ty once Jace was out of earshot. "Thanks for setting him on the task. He's been talking about horses for days now."

Ty took that as good news. If Jace cared so much about the stud, then he clearly cared about the ranch. Why bother with this research if he was going to leave it all behind?

At least there was one ray of brightness in his life right now.

Jace reappeared, the notebook now safely stashed away, and toed off his boots. "How's the barrel horse looking?"

That ray of brightness dimmed.

Unfortunately, while Red was quickly improving, the mare's recovery was still taking longer than expected. The location of the injury was in a terrible spot. There wasn't a lot of blood flow where the tendon was located because the leg was so narrow. While he expected the pressure point therapy was helping Red recover at a quicker pace than he expected, it wasn't working at the pace he had promised.

Problem was, he didn't know how to tell Ella or Jace.

Jace was expecting the success of the therapy to set up the ranch as a profitable vet practice. Ella was expecting to make it to the NFR.

"It's going," he hedged, keeping it vague. "She's healing well." Just not on their original timeline.

Footfalls echoed on the front porch and seconds later, Gus walked in, interrupting the conversation.

Never had Ty been more grateful for an interruption. He smiled hello, then watched as Gus's dark eyes landed on Colton and the smile on her face lit up the entire room.

Envy chased by a deep sense of loneliness shot through him as Gus headed straight to Colton and kissed him full on the mouth.

He liked both Hailey and Gus, and he felt his brothers had truly won out with the amazing women in their lives. Hailey and Gus clearly brought out the best in his brothers, and Colton and Jace both looked happy whenever they were around.

It was just that every time he saw how happy the two couples were, Ty felt even more alone.

"Hi." The feminine voice behind him was hesitant.

Whirling around, he spotted Ella, standing awkwardly at the threshold of the front door. Her chin was tilted down, her dark hair pulled over one shoulder like a curtain protecting her. The skin around her eyes was pinched, and she looked like she hadn't slept in days.

Ty could feel everyone's eyes turn to him.

"I didn't mean to just drop in. Or I guess I did. Gus took me grocery shopping, and I asked…" She waved her hands, looking around, as though realizing that she and Ty were the center of attention. "If she'd mind bringing me over to talk with you for a few minutes."

She was taking her horse.

Probably an irrational thought, but nonetheless, it was the first thing that popped into his head. After all, why would she want to keep her horse with the vet she despised?

The thing was, he needed to keep Red here. He needed to follow through with the therapy and prove that it did work.

He should have thought twice before blowing up at her the other day. He could have just accepted her judgment, swallowed his pride, and put on a front until Red was healed.

But no, he had to give her what-for.

"Fine," he growled, his mood now sour. "Let's talk outside." Away from the prying eyes and ears. He motioned out the front door.

"I'll be here when you're ready to head home," Gus called to Ella as he followed the dark-haired cowgirl out the door. The steps were probably a little treacherous on crutches, but he stopped himself from offering help, and she didn't ask.

He led her over to the barn where they could get some privacy before turning to her.

"Can we make this short? It's been a long day and I still have some things to do." Granted his to-do list was laundry and coordinating with Colton and Jace when to move the bull out with the cows, but she didn't need to know that.

"I won't keep you long." She looked up, her lips pressed flat, and her eyes serious. "I want to apologize."

"Great." He clapped his hands together. Apology done, time to wrap this up.

"There's more," she said softly, and something about the misery in her tone stopped him from heading back to the house. "I judged you by what I expected from someone like you rather than by the actions you showed. While I can't take back the past, I am sorry for my shortsightedness and for hurting you. You, of all people, don't deserve that. You have been nothing but wonderful to me, and I want to let you know that my perception of you was completely wrong."

The barrier he had mentally planted around himself crumbled a little at her words.

Her eyes were big and soft as she looked at him. "I'm not expecting you to forgive me, but I thought I could share with you why I was acting the way I did."

"Shoot." He shrugged, trying to look like he didn't care.

Only he did care.

Gazing off into the distance, she took a breath before turning back to him, her expression resigned. "I'm sure you overheard at the dance that Jeff and I had a...thing going. I hadn't realized that he and Lindsey were still together. It's one more issue between Lindsey and me." Heat bloomed on her cheeks. "Anyway, Jeff led me to believe he and Lindsey were no longer together, so we started hooking up."

"Okay," he said, his interest piqued. How Ella could fall for someone like Jeff was beyond him.

"At first, it was fun," Ella continued. "And so easy to fall into it. He'd come over at night, sweet and charming. And honestly, it was flattering that a handsome cowboy was interested in me. I never thought someone in this town would actually be interested in me."

That was bullshit. There were plenty of guys—

"Turns out, he wasn't interested in me. He just wanted sex," Ella continued. "I started asking why we weren't going out on dates, or why he didn't want me to hang out with him at his place. Turns out it was because he and Lindsey had not broken up. It took me weeks to piece it all together. One night, he came over, and his phone started buzzing like mad. He kept ignoring the calls and put the phone on silent. A few minutes later, Lindsey showed up at my door."

Ella's jaw was tight, as she swallowed.

Ty felt his muscles bunch as Ella struggled to say her next words. The next time he saw Jeff, he wasn't going to be so nice.

"Lindsey and Jeff were still together. I was the side piece." Her voice had become robotic. As though she were trying to recite the facts without the emotion, but everything about her curled forward, as though protecting a wound. Her eyes glazed over, and she looked like she wanted to imagine the whole situation away.

"I was furious." Her voice cracked, and he moved forward. Ella moved back. "No, I need to get this out. A few days later, I drove to his house and demanded to know why he would do something like that. You know what he did? What he said?"

No, and Ty was pretty positive that he was going to destroy Jeff once he heard.

"He shrugged. The asshole actually shrugged and asked

what else did I expect. I got the most I was ever going to from someone like him, and I should be happy with it."

Ty saw red. His jaw ached as he clenched his fists. If he ever saw Jeff again, he was going to make sure that guy regretted the day he set his sights on Ella.

Ella was sniffing, her nose and cheeks red with suppressed tears. More than anything, he wanted to pull her close and just hold her. Of course she deserved better. Far better than someone like Jeff.

"You didn't deserve that," he said vehemently.

"I'm surprised you would say that after our blowup the other day." Ella let out a dry laugh that sounded hollow. "I just…" She wrapped her arms around herself. "I guess after Lindsey and Jeff, I didn't want to feel like a fool again. I was determined to prove to everyone I was worth something. I wasn't some bottom-of-the-barrel person without any feelings or dreams. I wasn't less than."

He grabbed her shoulders. "Of course you aren't less than. You're better than either of them." He would pick her any day of the week.

Ella gave a wry smile. He couldn't help but notice that her knuckles around her crutch grips were white.

"Anyway," she continued. "I've been attracted to you for years. I had a crush on you back in high school, and I guess it never really went away." She let out another laugh, only this felt shy. "But after Jeff, I wasn't willing to put myself out there again. I didn't mean to hold onto a high school grudge, it was just so much easier to protect myself by holding onto old hurts. So, I did. And in return, I've hurt a really great guy who didn't deserve it."

"I get it," he muttered. Did it bother him? Yes. Did he understand? Yes. Moving close, he wrapped his arms around her before she could escape. "You didn't deserve that. You are not lesser than the Jeffs, or Lindseys, of the world. You're just as good. Better."

"Not better," she sniffed. "If I was better, I wouldn't have hurt you."

"But I get why," he started. Ella pressed her cheek against his shoulder, the movement feeling strangely natural. As though she were meant to always be there. She let her head rest against him for a minute before she pushed back.

"I want to prove to you that I'm not hiding away. That I can move on."

As far as he was concerned, she didn't need to prove anything to him. He understood. "Don't feel like you have to—"

"Yes, I do," she insisted. "This may sound a bit dumb, but trivia night is coming up this week."

Trivia night at the Last Saloon was a popular monthly occurrence. He went on occasion, and even saw Ella there once or twice. He hadn't been planning on going, but he was curious where she was going with this. "Okay, what does that have to do with proving you've moved on?"

"I wondered if you'd want to go with me. I normally go with Jordan and we keep to ourselves, but I can go with you, hang out with you and your friends." She shrugged, as though it explained the rest. When he didn't move, she added, "It shows I'm willing to put myself out there for you. Despite the gossip, despite being afraid I could be hurt again, I want to show I can move past old hurts."

"I get it." And he did. "You want to prove that you aren't hiding anymore."

She bit her lip. "For you. I want to prove that to you."

"Why for me?" he found himself asking.

Her cheeks turned a brilliant shade of red, and his pulse quickened in response. He leaned forward, closer to her, wanting to hear whatever she had to say that made her blush like that.

Then she spoke the words he'd been craving for years.

"Because I still like you," she said.

CHAPTER NINE

"I'M SORRY, YOU agreed to what?" Jordan's voice shouted through the phone in shock and excitement.

Ella yanked the cell away from her ear as Jordan continued to shout and put it on speaker to save her eardrum from future abuse. In the background, she could hear the chatter of people and the clink of dishes. Jordan's conference was clearly in full swing.

"I know. Is this crazy? I feel crazy." Ella chewed her lip as she studied her reflection. She felt like she was trying too hard. It was her brace's fault. It was hard to find something casual and comfortable to wear over a brace.

And maybe she wanted to look just a little bit nice for Ty.

"I just want to show that I can put myself out there," Ella continued, twisting in the mirror.

"I see," Jordan said. "I knew he wasn't as bad as you painted him."

Ella cringed. She really had been a complete idiot when it came to Ty. Jordan echoing her earlier sentiments only proved it further. It was likely she had lost her chance with Ty, but at least she'd have a better idea after tonight.

"What are you wearing?" Jordan asked.

"I'm wearing a black tank dress with that cropped denim

jacket you got me for my birthday."

"And wear your hair down. You won't regret it," Jordan advised.

"Don't read too much into this." She pulled a pair of black flats over her feet and slipped the two silver bangles her mom gave her when she graduated community college over her wrist. "We're friends working through the past."

Jordan snorted. "Have you kissed him?"

Despite the fact her friend couldn't see her, Ella could feel her face start to burn. Good thing Jordan was away at a conference instead of in the same room.

"I'll take that as a yes," Jordan said smugly when Ella didn't answer. "Have you told your dad yet?"

Jordan may as well have dumped ice on her good mood.

"There isn't anything to tell yet." For all she knew, after tonight, Ty would only be interested in a friendship. And she would take it.

"Does your dad even know that Ty is working on your horse?" Jordan followed up.

"Yeah, about that..." Ella said sucking air between her teeth. Jordan had a point. She needed to tell her dad. It was better he heard it from her rather than through some long-distance gossip. "I'll tell him this week. I hope he doesn't kill me."

"Well, if the rumors are true, you and Ty sound like you'll be hooking up soon," Jordan predicted.

Ella cocked her head at the phone.

"How are you hearing the Garnet Valley rumors? I thought your conference was in Nevada." Ella hadn't realized the town gossip crossed state lines.

"Please," Jordan laughed. "My family lives in Garnet Valley, and I've only been gone a week. My mom heard from your neighbor at her last grocery run."

Leave it to Ms. Minna.

Ella stared at her reflection in the mirror. She had on light makeup, her hair was down, and in the black tank and denim jacket, she was the most dressed up she had been since the dance at the Dillon rodeo.

She was really going to do it. She was going to put herself out there. Not as a girl from the wrong end of town. Not as a winner. Just as Ella.

A wave of panic slowly washed over her. What if tonight was a complete disaster and people didn't care who she was?

If felt like she was ripping herself open and showing off her weaknesses for the town to see.

And Ty was definitely one of her weaknesses.

"I don't know if I can do this," she said quickly to Jordan.

"Of course you can. If you're second-guessing the dress, don't," Jordan said, as though reading her mind. "Just give Ty a chance and follow through on your word. I think Ty will surprise you."

Ella chewed her lip.

"Promise you'll wear the dress?" her friend asked, her voice calm and soothing.

Ella sighed and pulled her hair over her shoulder. "I'm wearing the dress."

"Good. That cowboy is going to be a puddle at your feet," Jordan said smugly.

That didn't help her nerves one bit.

ELLA LOOKED STUNNING.

Ty sucked in a breath and rubbed his jaw as she came out of the house, free of crutches, wearing a soft-looking black dress and a denim jacket. Her dark hair fell in waves over her shoulders and curled around her breasts.

The brace still restricted her movement, but that didn't detract from how beautiful she was.

"Is everything okay?" Ella asked as he walked her to the truck.

He could barely breath, she was so pretty.

"I'm fine."

The corners of Ella's mouth pulled down for a second, then she shrugged and hoisted herself up into the truck. "Thanks for picking me up. I'm still feeling a bit off with the crutches gone. I guess I was more dependent on them than I had realized."

Her hand rested on the console between them as he maneuvered the truck to the Last Saloon. Her long fingers were slightly spread, as though waiting for him to twine his hand with hers.

It was only that reminder that tonight was her trial run that stopped him.

The Last Saloon was crowded, as it always was for trivia night. The event gave the community a chance to get out, socialize, and compete. Those who didn't like trivia came down for the wings and dancing afterward. Either way, the monthly night was a hit with the town.

Ty pushed the heavy front door open and was greeted by an onslaught of conversation and laugher. Crowds weren't his thing, but he did enjoy trivia night.

He maneuvered around the crowd, weaving his way through the bodies as he looked for familiar faces. Ella stayed close behind him. Both of his brothers were supposed to be here, as well as a few friends from around town.

A warm delicate hand pressed lightly on his back, and a flare of heat rocked through him.

"Over there," Ella said, leaning close so he could hear her above the conversation. The nearness of her lips and breath against the shell of his ear had him suppressing a groan. Looking in the direction she pointed, he spotted his brothers, their ladies, and a couple of longtime friends, and, of course, Lindsey.

If Ella had anything to say against the other woman, she kept it to herself as he grabbed her hand and led her to the table.

If anyone was surprised to see him with Ella, no one said a word. Gus and Hailey greeted Ella immediately, wrapping their arms around her in quick hugs.

Ty smiled to himself as Ella looked a little surprised at the fondness but hugged them back. He seated himself next to Colton and pulled a chair close for Ella.

"Ella," someone in the crowd called. "It's good to see you."

Ella's hands on the table curled into themselves, then relaxed as she turned around and smiled at the woman who called out.

"Did you ever come to trivia?" Ty asked after Ella exchanged small talk with the woman. Another person called her name, and Ella waved back.

"On occasion with Jordan, but we'd typically sit in a corner and eat wings." Ella grimaced and ducked her head, her dark hair gleaming softly in the dim light. "I guess I was hiding away. I had no idea people would be happy to see me."

A few more people stopped by to say hi. Out of the corner of his eye, he spotted Lindsey giving his dark-haired beauty long glances. After hearing about the prom prank, he couldn't help feeling a little irritated at Lindsey's youthful immaturity but forced himself to let it go. Lindsey had changed, and honestly, so had he and Ella.

He leaned back, looking for the waitress, the move shifting his body closer to Ella's. The coconut scent of her shampoo managed to rise about the smells of beer and wings, arresting his attention as she pulled her hair forward and over her chest.

"Everyone is staring," she muttered softly under her breath. Her fingers twisted her long length of hair into a rope.

Indeed, there were quite a few people sneaking glances at them. Some were flat-out staring. Something told him the recent town gossip wasn't helping. And honestly, part of him was thrilled to be seen out with Ella.

He shrugged. "Let them stare. We know what this is. Let them think whatever they want."

Ella looked ready to say something but seemed to think better of it. He leaned closer to ask what was on her mind, but Colton interrupted.

"Ella, it's good to see you. I was worried when you didn't

show up the last couple of days. It looks like you lost your crutches and are closer to recovery," Colton said.

Ella's shoulders relaxed. "I did. Just a few more weeks, and I should be back in the saddle. I can't wait to be riding Red again."

Ty stiffened. Red was not on track, and the more days that passed, the more concerned he became the horse wouldn't be ready for the NFR.

Then, before he, or either of his brothers, could say a word, their waitress, April, stopped by. Ella's knee pressed into his as she turned to place her order.

The young woman eyed them both with unconcealed interest as she took their orders.

"Glad to see you guys here tonight," April said, gracing them with a wide, friendly smile. "Jace and Hailey, I've heard some people have been studying all week to get one up on you two. Are you ready for tonight?"

Ty snorted. Jace and Hailey usually teamed up for trivia, and last month, they destroyed everyone in the room.

"She's the genius behind this operation," Jace said, pointing at his wife fondly. "So the pressure is on her, not me."

Hailey gave Jace a friendly smack. Ella laughed softly next to him as she watched the banter between his brother and sister-in-law.

"I'm not sure why everyone is talking up Jace and Hailey. I'm just as bad-ass at trivia as those two," Ty said, smiling at his oldest brother so he knew Ty was joking.

"You've got to keep these Hartmans in check," Gus said to Ella. "Or they get big egos like Ty here."

Ella snorted. "It's hard to keep that vet ego in check."

She laughed as he rolled his eyes.

"The only egos here are Jace's and Colton's. I've got mine under control." He reached up and tugged a lock of her dark hair, wrapping it around his fingers.

"Dear god," Ella chuckled. "Fine. Fine. You have a miniscule ego. I have to grab a magnifying glass to find it."

He couldn't help himself and was soon laughing with her.

When he looked at Gus, her eyebrows were raised, and a smile played on her lips, like she knew a secret he didn't.

Clearing his throat, he unwound Ella's silky hair from his fingers and dropped his hands to the table. However, despite his best efforts, he was finding this laughing, friendly Ella impossible to resist. He wanted to be closer to her, to touch her. Her leg brushed against his, the contact ebbing and flowing along with the conversation.

He wanted more.

Leaning close, he murmured in her ear, "Are you having fun?"

Ella's face turned a soft, pretty shade of pink under her olive skin. "Yeah. Your family is great."

Her green eyes caught his, and suddenly their surroundings seemed to disappear. It didn't matter that they were in a bar, or the crowd was so loud that they had to shout to talk to each other, or that dozens of eyes were on them, it felt like it was just them.

"Here are your beers!" April stopped just behind him and Ella, and with smooth movements, started unloading drinks from the black tray she carried.

Ella pulled away to give the blond waitress room to set the drinks down, but her knee still touched his. The contact was so innocent, yet it was driving him up the wall.

"And the trivia supplies," the waitress added as she dropped trivia cards and pencils on the table.

"Thanks, April," Ella said as she grabbed her beer and held it up. "Thanks everyone for letting me sit with you guys."

Her face was flush as she said the words, but Ty knew that she was saying more than just thanks to his family.

"Of course," Jace said. He leaned across the table. "By the way, do you know anything about horse bloodlines?"

Ty snorted. Jace, while still researching a stud, was now looking into brood mares as well.

Ella gave him a weird look. "Sure? Why do you ask?"

Which started a long conversation about Jace's job to find a stud for the ranch. Ella threw in some of her insight, while Jace took notes on his phone, until trivia was announced.

"Team with me?" Ella asked Ty as people started to quiet down.

"Of course, partner," he said, grinning at her. He dropped an arm on the back of her chair, pulling himself closer.

Ella flushed and took a drink of her beer. Ty watched with interest as he sipped the beer he planned to savor for the night.

Out of the corner of his eye, he saw Lindsey get up and excuse herself. Grabbing her jacket and her purse, the other woman pushed through the crowd, not once looking back. It appeared she wasn't planning on returning either.

That wasn't like Lindsey. She normally said goodbye. At least to him.

"Everything okay?" he asked his buddies down at the end of the table.

They both shrugged. "She said something came up."

Ty turned and watched her until she exited out the front door, her shoulders stiff as the door closed after her. Hopefully, everything was okay.

He tapped his thumb against the table, a static rhythm until Ella quietly slid her hand across the table and flattened her fingers against his.

"Go catch up with her," Ella said softly.

He looked at her face, trying to discern if there was any sense of sarcasm or envy in her voice. But instead, all he found was her looking at him with wide, concerned eyes.

He hated having a friend hurt. Grabbing his phone from his pocket, he shot her a message. Lindsey was a big girl. Whatever was going on with her clearly had something to do with Ella. Shifting in his seat, he wondered just how long he'd been missing Lindsey's snide comments.

"All right, ladies and gents," the announcer called. "It's that time. The one you've been waiting for. It's Trivia Night!"

He turned to his trivia partner, who smiled happily up at him, and all troubles were forgotten.

JACE AND HAILEY not only kicked butt at trivia, they destroyed all competition.

Ella shook her head as she watched them rack up the points round after round. Jace watched his wife with quiet pride as

Hailey furiously scrawled the answers to the trivia questions.

It was cute really. If she and Ty weren't losing so bad.

"I'm sorry I ever said you had a big ego," Ella whispered to Ty, leaning close so he could hear. The scent of pine and leather washed over her. "Jace and Hailey take trivia to a whole new level."

"Tell me about it," Ty laughed. The sound was low and gravelly, and her body reacted instantly, heating as she swayed closer to him. Her belly felt like a molten pool, and her panties were damp from the constant contact with the sexy vet sitting next to her.

It was driving her wild.

As soon as trivia wrapped up, the crowds began to disperse, some heading home for the night as others hit the dance floor or the pool tables. The jukebox was turned on, and music began to blast from the overhead speakers.

Jace and Hailey were laughing with each other, faces bright from another trivia win, and Colton smiled as he offered Gus his hand. Seconds later, both couples left the table to dance.

What happened now? Hailey pushed her trivia card to the middle of the table before giving him a tentative smile. She didn't know if Ty planned to stick around or if he wanted to go.

Either way, she was game. Tonight turned out to be more fun than she was expecting. Why had she waited so long to put herself out there? It was so worth it.

She pressed her face against Ty's shoulder and squeeze his forearm with her free hand.

"What's that for?" he asked, his voice a low rumble.

"Thanks for getting me out of my shell," she said.

"Any time." He slid his hand over hers, trapping her fingers against his arm.

People were passing by their table, and she could see the sidelong glances. Biting her lip, she fought her body's urge to snuggle in closer and instead pulled away.

If Ty noticed anyone staring, he didn't show it. His leg pressed against hers, thigh to thigh, calf to calf, the denim of his pants creating a slight friction against the bare skin of her leg.

Ty finished the last drops of water he had started half an hour ago and set the glass on the table. "I hate to do this, but I have a surgery first thing tomorrow and should probably head home. I can give you a ride if you want, or if you prefer to stay, I'm sure Jace or Colton can help you get back."

"I'm ready to head home," she said. The evening, while fun, was beginning to wear her down.

And she wanted a bit more time with Ty.

Ty stood and helped her out of her chair, wrapping his warm hand around hers to steady her. He didn't let go as he led her through the bar, going slow enough that she could keep up even with her brace.

They finally broke through the crowd and pushed through the door into the cool night air. Ella took a deep breath of clean mountain air mixed with the sweet scent of fields and baked dirt roads. The smell of her hometown during the early fall.

Ty put his hand at the small of her back as they headed to his truck across the street. There was a bite in the air, and Ella shivered in her little denim jacket.

The ride back to her place was silent. Tense. Ty had been

flirting with her all night, and not knowing what to expect only made her crave him more. He could just drop her off and drive home. Or he could stay a while. Just the hope that something would happen had her body humming with anticipation.

Ty parked in her driveway.

"Wait here," he said before walking around her side of the truck to help her out.

His fingers lingered on her waist after she was steady on the ground, and he didn't immediately move away. His hooded eyes were drinking her in, and her body arched in response.

Her knees felt like liquid and her body seemed too heavy to support itself. Bracing her hands against Ty's chest, she leaned into him.

"Thanks for agreeing to this," she said, her voice low. "I couldn't have done this without you. I would have felt like everyone was laughing at me."

"No one was laughing at you." Ty's voice was firm, gravelly. His brows pulled together, studying her carefully as he gently ran his thumb along her cheekbone.

Her breath hitched at the contact as lust surged through her.

"You were gorgeous tonight." Dropping his head, Ty's lips followed the path of his thumb, trailing soft, gentle kisses along her cheekbone, then jawline. "I hope you realize that."

"Ty?" Her voice was breathy, practically a moan.

"Damn it," he growled, then pulled her close.

His mouth found hers, hot and insistent. Like he couldn't handle himself any longer. His tongue licked the seam of her lips, and she opened to him, yielding against his slightest pressure.

Before she knew it, her back was against the truck door, her legs parted, and she was straddling his thigh, her skirt up around her waist.

And she didn't care. The cool evening air was a delicious contrast to the heat pooling between her legs and the rough denim that clad Ty's thigh.

His mouth was hot as he took control, bracing his arms on either side of her as though if he touched her, he'd lose all control.

She wanted him to lose that control. Her fingers went to his shirt, pulling it out of the waistband, and she was immediately rewarded with the smooth skin of his stomach. She traced the lines of his abdominal muscles, following the path until they disappeared into the waistband of his jeans.

Tucking her fingers into the band, she nipped at his lower lip before going to his jeans button.

"Ella," Ty groaned. His biceps flexed, and he broke the kiss. "Damn."

Emotion battled over his face as though he were trying to restrain himself and was struggling to do so. He dropped his head, tracing a line of kisses along her jaw then collarbone, as though he couldn't help himself.

"Want to come in?" There was no mistaking the throatiness in her voice and what the invitation was really for.

Ty froze, his mouth against her neck. Then, with a groan, he straightened, bracing his body against his arms.

"I can't. Not tonight." There was a hint of regret in his voice.

She froze, trapped in the cage of his arms. "Did I do something—"

"No," he interrupted. "I just… Not yet." He ran a hand over his face. "It's not anything you did tonight. Tonight was amazing. I just don't trust that this isn't a one-time thing. I want this to be more. I really do, but only if you want more than one night of fun."

If she wanted more than one night of fun? Of course she did. That seemed like an obvious answer.

But clearly there was more to it than he was saying. Only earlier this week she had hurt him, and after learning about his mom leaving, something told her that he was as wary about letting people in as she was. While she couldn't fix the break with his mom, she could try to weld together the pieces she had broken. Somehow, she had to prove how serious she was, then hope that she hadn't destroyed whatever chance she did have.

Ty pushed away, rubbing at his jaw. His body was hard and rigid, and she was finding it impossible to look away.

"I'll stop by tomorrow to feed. Does that work?" he asked.

She nodded, suddenly feeling a little foolish.

"Just think about what you want," Ty said, lust steeped in his voice. "We can talk about it later."

Then with one last, light kiss on her lips, he walked her to her front door, waited until she was inside, and then headed back to his truck.

From her living room window, she watched him drive away. As she prepared for bed, she found herself wondering if now that she wanted more, Ty had decided he had enough.

CHAPTER TEN

ELLA WOKE UP late the following day, the sheets twisted around her legs, and her body aching for Ty.

Yet another dream about the handsome cowboy.

The fact that he left right after that mind-blowing kiss didn't help at all. It had left her feeling hot, and needy, and...well, a little hurt. She understood why he didn't want to go further. Of course she had no one to blame but herself.

However, after last night, with the fun they had and the way he wouldn't stop looking at her, she had hoped *something* would happen.

Apparently, she was wrong.

Maybe she should focus on being grateful that Ty was still working on Red, and he was helping her be ready for the NFR. The kisses were just bonuses...that left her wishing for more.

Rubbing the sleep out of her eyes, she shoved the thought to the back of her mind and pushed to the edge of the bed. Strapping on the brace, she threw a skirt and tank over the bralette and cotton underwear she had slept in and headed into the kitchen.

Thanks to the grocery trip with Gus, her kitchen was stocked, and she had something to look forward to besides peanut butter. Putting on a kettle for tea, Ella grabbed a couple eggs from the tiny almond-colored fridge to scramble.

Humming under her breath, she glanced out the kitchen window as she mixed the eggs in a glass bowl. The sun was just above the mountains, greeting her with a beautiful, clear day. The weather looked perfect to sit outside and enjoy the morning as she sipped tea.

Propping her front door open, she headed to her porch to set up the little table and chair she used for such occasions.

Once the table was set up, she glanced over to make sure Ty had fed her horse and pony. Sure enough, the open bale from yesterday was shorter, and the two horses—

Ella blinked.

The two horses should have been at the trough eating, but there were no horses in sight.

Ty probably stopped by half an hour ago. Forty-five minutes at most. Mickey and Maverick should have still been eating.

But that didn't explain two missing animals.

Or the open gate.

Blood rushed from her head as she stared at the gate. Had Ty let her horses out?

No, that didn't make sense. Ty wouldn't do something like that.

Scrambling down the three worn porch steps, she hurried to the pen as fast as she could.

Nope, her eyes were not deceiving her. Mickey and Maverick were not in their pen. In fact, they were nowhere in sight.

Panic squeezed at her lungs as she looked the gate over, and the reason for her horses' escape became clear. The gate latch dangled from the steel eyebolt embedded on the fence post, and a broken chain hung from the gate.

Her stomach gave a sickening lurch then contracted into a tight ball.

Oh dear god, no. Not Mickey. Not Maverick. Maverick wasn't even her pony. Yet.

What if something happened to them?

Her heart leapt to her throat and pulsed full and hard, making her feel weak and nauseous.

Slowly, she turned around, willing her horses to show up.

They were nowhere in sight. Not in her tiny yard, not in the pen, not even in her neighbor's yard.

Heading to the road, her movements stilted by her weak leg and stiff brace, Ella peered down the street in both directions.

No horses.

Shit. Shit. Shit.

There was no way she could look for the horses on her own. Sure she could drive her truck around until she spotted them, but how the heck was she supposed to catch them once she found them? Limp over to them with a halter? Mickey would no doubt turn tail and run. And the pony would likely follow.

What if they got hit by a truck?

What if Mickey got injured? Then she'd have zero barrel horses. She would literally be back at square one.

She rushed back to her house as fast as her legs could carry her, wishing she could run. Grabbing her cell, she fumbled to unlock it, and then dialed the first person that came to mind.

He answered after the third ring.

"Ty, the horses are gone!" she shouted into the phone, too

panicked to care if she sounded unhinged.

"I'm sorry, what?" he asked, his voice much calmer than hers.

"My horses! Were they here when you came by this morning?" She knew she sounded crazy but she was scared for her mare and her pony.

"Of course they were there. I would have told you if they weren't," Ty said, concern filling his voice.

"Well, they're gone now, and I have no clue where. When did you feed them?"

"Over an hour ago. I had to get to the clinic early today."

Ella closed her eyes. Of course. He'd mentioned the surgery appointment he had.

"When did you notice them missing?" he demanded.

"Just now."

"Alright," he said, his voice resolute. "Let me call the other vet and see if he can take on my cases for the morning. Then I'll go look for them."

Ella hung up the phone and headed back outside, grabbing a halter as she did.

If anyone could help her out of a bind, it was Ty. She had no doubt in that, but until he was here, she was going to look for her horses herself.

IT HAD TAKEN the other vet twenty minutes to show up, and after running through the situation and thanking him a zillion times over, Ty was in his truck, driving through town, eyes peeled for free-ranging equines.

Ella had called twice more, telling him that she was driving around the back roads by her place looking for the horses.

He told her to head home in case her horses showed up. He could tell by her long silence that she wasn't thrilled with the idea, but she reluctantly agreed when he pointed out that if they came home, someone needed to be there.

Thirty minutes later, he had no clue where the horses could have ended up. Despite driving through all the bordering neighborhoods, he had not seen hide nor hair of either Mickey or Maverick. He called a few neighboring ranches, but no one had seen any new herd additions, though they promised to keep their eyes open and would let him and Ella know if they found the renegade equines.

Ty hoped Ella knew how supported she was during this.

Forty-five minutes later, the horses were still missing, and he was running out of ideas. He was driving up and down the streets of yet another neighborhood when his phone buzzed on the passenger seat.

Snapping it off the seat, Ty pressed it to his ear.

"Hello," he answered, using the calm vet voice he used when the situation was out of his control.

"Hey, Ty." It was one of the neighbors he had called earlier. "Have you happened to check out the downtown area?"

He had not. In terms of town traffic, it was a busier area, so he had assumed the horses would avoid the noise and chaos.

"Nope, why do you ask?"

"Well, I stopped by Dave's Burgers to pick up lunch for the crew, and there's a horse and a small pony hanging out in the drive-thru," the neighbor drawled, the humor evident in his voice.

Ty hit the brakes, stopping in the middle of the road. Thank god it was a quiet street. "They're at the drive-thru?"

"Yes, siree. The high school kids are having quite a time with their visitors. One kid is hanging out the drive-thru window to pet the pony."

If he hadn't been so worried about Ella and how panicked she must be, this situation would have been funny. "Any chance you happen to have a halter on you?"

"Yep. I'll see if I can catch them. That pony is an ornery little one, though."

By the time he got to Dave's Burgers, Mickey was caught, and the pony was standing idly by, grazing at some grass near the edge of the parking lot. Clearly Maverick avoided all attempts to be captured.

The neighbor, an older cowboy with a full gray beard sat on his open tailgate, eating a burger and running his hand along Mickey's neck as the mare nosed at the bit of hay left in the bed of the old ranch truck.

"You two are in big trouble," Ty said after he parked his truck and got out to thank the neighbor.

"You good to take them back?" the older cowboy asked.

"I'm good," Ty said, taking the horse from the neighbor and promising to return the halter later in the evening. The neighbor waved and drove off, leaving Ty with a horse and a strong-willed pony.

Ella's place was five-ish miles from Dave's Burgers. A quick drive in a truck. And a much different scenario walking, especially wearing cowboy boots. Even if his Ariats were well broken-in. It was one thing to stand in them at the clinic all day. It was another thing entirely to walk in them for five miles down cracked concrete sidewalks on a warm day.

Yet here he was. There was no way he could ask Ella to hook up her gooseneck trailer and drive over. He didn't want to risk her straining her knee. And honestly, he didn't want to hang out at the burger joint for longer than necessary. If Maverick spooked and ran off, it would make the situation even messier.

The only other option was to jump on Mickey's back and ride over, but he wasn't going to get on a horse he wasn't familiar with without a saddle.

At least the two looked tired from their big adventure.

He talked a couple of the high school kids he knew at Dave's into dropping his truck off at Ella's, and then led Mickey out of the parking lot. Maverick stood his ground, refusing to budge, until Ty and Mickey rounded the corner. Then with his little pony head held high, he trotted after them as quick as his tiny strides would take him.

Two miles in, the horses were over the whole ordeal and were trying to stop every few feet for bites of grass. His feet ached, and his low back was complaining. He just ducked his head and kept walking, focusing his attention on the rhythmic clacking of hooves against the hard concrete. He made a mental note to check their hooves and joints before he left Ella's place to make sure the impact on the hard surfaces didn't cause any damage.

Four miles in, the fall sun felt hotter than hell, and he was sweating through his shirt. But he just kept walking.

The thought that kept him going was that Ella trusted him with her horses. Out of everyone she could have called—Jordan, her neighbors, his brothers, Gus—she had picked him.

Finally, he rounded the last corner and spotted Ella's house, his truck parked out in front, a short distance away.

Relief washed over him. He was sweating and exhausted. His knees ached, and there were several blisters forming on his feet. But the look on Ella's face as he led the duo onto her property made the whole thing worth it.

His heart started hammering in his chest as her pinched face relaxed into an expression of relief. She hurried off the porch to greet them.

"Shame on you both," she scolded the tiny herd as she ran a hand over Mickey's body. She inspected both horses, her eyes sharp, and he knew she was checking for injury.

"I'll check them before I leave as well," he reassured her as she ran her hands over both horse and pony.

Once she was satisfied the animals were okay, he led Mickey into the pen, Maverick following, and let them loose. The two went straight for the hay in the trough, their heads drooping.

He spotted the broken gate latch as Ella grabbed a bit of baling twine and tied the gate closed with a couple loops and a half-hitch knot. He made a mental note to buy a new latch and fix the gate tomorrow morning when he stopped by.

Ella turned, and before he knew what was happening, she cupped her hands around his jaw, pulled his face down to hers, and kissed him.

It was a press of her lips. Nothing that should have been sensual, or sexual, but the way her mouth lingered on his just a second longer than he had expected had him instantly hard.

"Thank you," she whispered, her voice husky. "I knew you would find my horses."

She knew he would.

Trusted that he would.

Had reached out to him because she had faith he would find them.

And that was his undoing.

With a groan, he wrapped an arm around her waist, cupped the back of her head, and hauled her close.

Her lips were warm, soft, and yielding, giving way to him like he had always imagined late at night, right before falling asleep when he couldn't stop thinking of her.

He grabbed the halter from her hand and tossed it on the small haystack. Her hand moved to his neck, pulling him closer as he braced her body against his. Her soft breasts pressed against his chest, the heat of the day and the heat of her body blending into one.

A moan escaped her, encouraging him to nip at her lower lip until she opened to him, allowing him access to her mouth, to taste the sugar and coffee on her tongue.

And he wanted more of her, to taste her skin, her body, to feel her moving against him. The little restraint he'd been exercising was fraying fast. It would have required superhuman strength to stop kissing her, touching her, and at the moment, he didn't have it. He was so tired of resisting her.

He traced the edge of her jaw with his thumb, memorizing

the soft skin before dropping his hands lower to fall to her shoulders, and then lower, tracing the cage of her ribs to the yielding curve of her waist before he slipped his hands under the edge of her shirt to feel the skin underneath.

What he found was absolute heaven. Soft, silky skin that felt as amazing as she smelled, driving him wild.

Her hands followed suit, tracing their own path down his chest, her fingers following the ridge of his abs before dipping under the line of his jeans.

All he could breathe was Ella, all he could taste was Ella, all he could feel was Ella. And it wasn't enough.

He nipped at her full upper lip before dropping his head to run his lips, then teeth, along her jaw, along the column of her throat, to her collarbone.

When he looked up, he was arrested by how gorgeous she was. Her face was flush, her lips full and puffy from his kisses, and her green eyes cloudy with lust.

He didn't want to hold back anymore.

Grazing his fingers along her jawline, he lowered his forehead against hers. "Do you want to invite me inside?"

HELL YES, SHE wanted to invite him inside. She thought he would never ask.

However, Ella looked over her shoulder at the tiny little trailer she grew up in, and hesitated. Right now, her stuff was everywhere, and the kitchen sink had dishes in it, and her bed wasn't even made.

Inviting him inside was like opening herself up to him a little bit more, showing him a huge piece of her life.

Was she planning on him seeing her bedroom?

Was she overthinking this?

Was she ready for this?

"You don't have to." Ty stepped back, breaking the current between them.

What was she thinking? If there was someone she trusted, it was Ty. The cowboy would take her as she was, no matter where she came from or where she was going.

"Don't go." She placed her hand on his chest. "I'd love for you to come in."

Ty cocked his head to the side. "You sure?"

She was. She wanted Ty with her right now.

"I'm a hundred percent certain," she insisted. Then her mouth was on his. His arms wrapped around her, walking her backward until her feet hit the bottom step of her porch. Slowly, she walked up them, one by one.

Desperate to feel his body against hers, she slipped her fingers under the edge of his white shirt and pressed her palms against the hard planes of his chest.

All she wanted was to see him shirtless. Right now.

She pulled him inside her home and closed the screen door behind her. Without wasting a second, her hands flew to the buttons of his shirt, pulling it open, revealing the strong planes of his upper body. She stepped back, taking him in, and her mouth went dry.

Holy chocolate covered in whipped cream.

It had clearly been years since she'd last seen Ty shirtless, because damn. The last time was during high school when she and her dad had helped Beau with a summer cattle drive. At the end of the ride, Ty and his friends had jumped into the water troughs to cool off. While the man had been droolworthy then, it was nothing compared to now. This was hot on a whole new scale.

She tried, honestly she tried, to keep her eyes on his, but the temptation proved to be too much. Her eyes kept drifting lower, like her rational mind had taken a hiatus from the situation. Her gaze drifted past his chin, to the defined collarbone that extended out to his developed shoulders and well-muscled chest.

Since she was already on the tour, she let her gaze drop lower. There was not an ounce of flab of the man. Every flex, every movement of his muscles screamed of hours of manual work that honed his body into a well-defined machine. There was a light sprinkling of hair across his chest, and then a patch that disappeared into the waistband of his jeans.

Catching her breath, she looked up at Ty's face, and caught the fleeting mix of emotions that flew across his face faster than the clouds gathering just before a storm.

"Ella." Ty ran his hand down her arm, his touch leaving a trail of fire across her bare skin. Under the hot, hazy look in his eyes, she felt open and vulnerable. She hadn't been with someone since Jeff, who had used her in the end.

This time was different. This was Ty. She trusted him and knew to her soul he would take care of her.

And she loved him for it.

Her heart skittered to a stop as she processed the thought.

But it was true. She loved him. For longer than she had expected.

Reaching up, she pressed her hand against his face, along his jaw, feeling the warmth of his skin and the stubble of his beard against her fingers. Then winding her fingers into his hair, she tilted his head down to hers and kissed him full and hard. All the years of frustration, fighting the attraction, and the endless denial that she put herself through poured out into one kiss.

Ty groaned against her lips, then before she could say a word, Ty picked her up and settled her on the laminate kitchen counter. His skin was hot under her hands as she spread her legs to pull him closer, fitting his hips between her thighs and pressing his hardening cock against her core.

The friction and heat were making her delirious.

"This isn't fair," Ty muttered against her lips.

"Hmm?" She was too busy exploring the ridges and trails of his body to even care about anything like fairness.

"That I'm shirtless, and you are not." He whispered the words before taking the shell of her ear in his teeth, grating against the sensitive skin, making her gasp and arch into him.

"That sounds like a problem you should solve." Her own voice was throaty.

Ty didn't miss a beat before he pulled her tank and bralette over her head. Her nipples pebbled at the sudden exposure, and her small breasts were swollen, aching for the feel of his hands against her. She braced her hands behind her, arching against him. Her breasts thrust forward, begging for attention.

She closed her eyes, savoring the feel of his breath against her skin as he ducked his head. He pressed his lips against the top of her breast. Each inhale, each pulse of her heart seemed to extend from her to him as he traced his mouth and tongue from the top of her breast to her nipple, where he scraped his teeth against one rosy pebble, and then the other.

Then, he was all over her, cupping her breasts, squeezing them, tasting them. His hands moved lower, clamping her in place as she rocked against him.

It was all instinct at this point, and every instinct wanted all their clothes off. She reached for his waistband, her fingers going straight for the metal button, followed by the zipper.

His cock sprang free, tenting the fabric of his boxer briefs. Ella shoved his jeans down his thighs, pushing them to the floor with her good leg.

Ty undid the zipper of her skirt. Wrapping an arm around her waist, he lifted her just enough for her to wriggle out of the skirt, leaving her in the pink cotton underwear she had slept in.

"Damn," Ty breathed. He dropped his head so her lips rested against the crown of his head. "I had always imagined what you looked like naked. The fantasy doesn't compare to the real deal."

"Really?" She wasn't even wearing fancy underwear. Just simple cotton.

"Not even close." He squeezed her waist and then was back to kissing her senseless.

Deeper into Ty she fell, until all she could think about was that last layer in between them and how many steps it would take to get to the bedroom.

As if reading her mind, Ty slipped his hands under her

butt, ready to scoop her off the counter. "Where's the bed-room?"

"Just down—"

A loud rap echoed through the small space.

"—the—"

Another loud rap.

She looked up to see her elderly neighborhood shading her eyes as she peered through the screen door.

"Oh gosh," Ella gasped. She went rigid.

Ty spun around, arms up, muscles flexed, in nothing but his underwear.

"Ms. Minna," Ella wheezed out as she scrambled to pull Ty in front of her with one hand and desperately search for her tank top with the other. "I'm sorry. Just a minute. I'm—"

She looked wildly around for her shirt that was no doubt on the floor. There was no way to grab it without Ty bending down or her getting off the counter. Either way, she would be forced to flash her neighbor, who was smiling like the sun had just broken through the clouds.

Giving up on her shirt, she gripped Ty with both hands to make sure he didn't move one way or another. Ms. Minna may have known her for most of her life, but the idea of her neighbor seeing her naked was more than she could handle. As it was, there was no way she could look Ms. Minna in the eye for the next two months at least.

"No apologies, sweetie," the other woman called. "I just wanted to let you know that your boyfriend here pulled up a little too far in his truck, and he's partially blocking my drive-way. Could he move his vehicle back a bit so I can do my grocery shop?"

She closed her eyes and suppressed a groan. No doubt this was moving to the top of Ms. Minna's list of weekly news to share.

"Oh, of course." There was a tremor in her voice. Whether it was from pure embarrassment or leftover heat between her and Ty, she didn't want to know. "Let us make ourselves, uh, presentable—"

"I'll be right out, Ms. Minna," Ty said, his voice a low growl that was still doing things to her.

Things that made her want to push Ms. Minna's request to the side for just fifteen more minutes…

No. Now was not the time.

The little old lady waved bye and walked away, a broad smile on her face.

Ella wanted nothing more than to disappear on the spot.

She felt exposed, embarrassed. Like every bit of emotion and heat was written on her face.

Ignoring Ty's hand, she slipped off the countertop and landed softly on the creaky floor. Grabbing her clothes from the floor, she yanked the shirt over her head and the skirt up her legs.

"Ella…" Ty was taking his sweet time pulling first one long leg, then the other into his jeans, as though he were giving her plenty of time to see every inch of man she was missing out on.

Every hard inch of the man.

"Your shirt is inside out."

She glanced down to see the seams sticking out and resisted the urge to fix her shirt. "It's fine."

"Suit yourself." Ty ran his hand over his head. "I better get out before Ms. Minna comes back over."

Then, before she could say another word, he was out the door.

There she stood, in the middle of her kitchen, partially dressed, the door wide open, and Ty walked out without a goodbye.

If the ground could open up and swallow her alive, she wouldn't complain. At the very moment, she felt incredibly foolish.

Maybe it was better to know now how he felt than to find out later, like she had with Jeff.

She didn't bother to look outside as she pulled her clothes into place and combed her fingers through her hair. There was no way she could watch him drive off without feeling down, so she closed her door behind him and went into her kitchen to grab a pint of ice cream. All the better to mope with.

She pulled open the freezer and went for the first carton she could find when a knock at the door stopped her.

Scrunching her brows together, she closed the freezer and headed slowly to the door.

Pulling the door open, her heart began that fluttering rhythm all over again.

Ty was on the porch, bracing his arms against the door-frame. A small smile played on his lips. "Did you really think I was going to leave you just like that?"

CHAPTER ELEVEN

ELLA WAS IN trouble. Neon signs with bells and whistles flashed and blared in her mind, warning that once she started down this path, there was no return.

At this very minute, she didn't care. All she wanted was Ty.

He dropped his head and kissed her, the contact warm and languid. The bells and warnings quieted to a buzz and then to nothing at all. Nothing except for the sound of the soft moans escaping her throat as Ty's hands worked his crazy magic on her body.

Any mess in the aftermath would be dealt with later. At the moment, nothing else mattered expect for the feel of Ty against her body.

"Bedroom?" Ty asked.

When she nodded, he picked her up and followed her directions down the short hall and to her tiny bedroom. Her room was a collection of odds and ends furniture she had gathered over the years—from her childhood to now. The simple white nightstand she got in middle school, the wood desk from high school, the curtains she sewed herself. The bed was the newest addition when she decided it was time to upgrade her mattress to something soft and comfortable.

Ty eased her onto the blue plaid sheets, her floral comforter tossed onto one side of the bed. He leaned into her, bracing his arms on either side of her as the scent of pine and leather and Ty surrounded her. Just being in the cage of his arms made her body swell and ache.

Pushing onto her elbows, she placed her mouth on his neck, running her tongue over his pulse, kissing right at the sensitive spot by his jaw.

Ty groaned, and dropped to his knees, his large hands spreading her legs to fit his torso between her thighs.

Her fingers were desperate to get him naked again. All that effort earlier gone to waste, but it wasn't going to waste this time. Never had she been so desperate to touch someone in her entire life. She *needed* to feel his bare skin against her own.

Her fingers worked the buttons through the holes of his shirt. How she managed to get his shirt off without ripping off the tiny buttons was beyond her. He pulled his mouth from hers and ran his warm lips along the column of her throat, as she pushed the shirt off his shoulders, giving her a full view of his upper body.

Pulling his hands free of his sleeves, he quickly hauled her close again, his hands just as desperate as hers.

She went for his jeans, undoing them and pulling them down in seconds flat.

"This hardly seems fair," Ty muttered against her lips. "Here I am naked again, and you're still dressed."

"Keep up, cowboy," she said, her voice low as she explored the ridges of his gorgeous body.

"Don't fight fair, do we?" he whispered in her ear before taking the shell of her ear in his teeth and tracing the rim with his tongue. She gasped and arched into him.

Ty pulled the tank over her head, his hands skimming her waist and ribs as he did. The bralette quickly followed in the path of her shirt. Completely bare, she arched up, thrusting her nipples toward him, begging for attention.

He pressed his lips against the top of her breast before tracing his mouth along her skin until she was shaking with need and barely able to stand.

Ty eased her back onto the bed, keeping his wide chest between her legs, and tracing his hands along the length of her thighs. His thumbs slowly moved oh-so-teasingly close to her warm core. They were so close to where she wanted him yet still too far away.

Shifting between her legs, Ty ran his mouth along her inner thigh, then up her body, across her abdomen and to the underside of her breasts. She laced her fingers in his hair, holding him close. His movements were slow, easy, savoring. She didn't want slow.

Reaching between them, she lightly circled the head of his cock with her fingertips before pressing her palm flat against the ridge.

Hissing with need, he ground against her palm. His eyes closed, clearly savoring the feel of her. The man was gorgeous. His face was flush and his lashes dark against his tan skin. She continued to move her hand gently up and down the length of him, circling his girth with her fingers, mesmerized by how Ty moved against her.

His hips arched toward her, completely out of his control.

"No way," he muttered, before he shifted down her body,

pulling his cock out of her grasp and then kneeling in front of her. Then his wet mouth descended on her folds, knocking the wind out of her. She nearly lost it right there.

While there hadn't been a lot of men in her past, there were enough. Never had any of them made her feel like this. Not with this connection that made every touch, every movement amplified, until all she could think of was the two of them and how he made her feel. The sound, the touch, the feel of the man trapping her body against his was the only man in this world she needed.

Her orgasm was building, and she dug her nails into his back as he ran his tongue along the length of her slit. She was seconds from losing it.

"Wait." Her voice sounded husky and foreign, even to her.

Ty pulled back, his dark brows furrowing together.

"I'm going to come before I'm ready," she panted.

A confident smirk crossed his face, sexy and sinful. "I'm good with that." He moved toward her again, but not before she stopped him.

"No, I want you inside of me. Please."

The lust in his eyes grew even hazier.

"And let's take this thing off." She motioned toward the brace.

"Your wish…" he said.

There was no way that taking a brace off should have made her wetter, but the way he moved along the length of her leg, his fingers and lips lingering on her skin, sucking and nipping as he undid each strap was driving her wild.

He was taking his sweet time, savoring the taste of her skin, driving her wild. Her body was quivering, her thighs pressing against his shoulders of their own accord.

Finally, the brace was off, and he set it gently on the ground.

"I'm going to kill you for that," Ella moaned as Ty helped her fully onto the bed, his lips finding her as she laid back, her hair pooling behind her.

Her skin felt hot and flush as he traced his fingers over the multitude of tan lines along her shoulders.

"Condom," she commanded.

"Right," Ty said.

She dove for her nightstand and pulled a small strip of condoms out of the top drawer and passed one to Ty. His fingers were shaking as he quickly sheathed himself. Then before she knew it, he was straddling her hips, nudging at her opening.

Her nails dug into his shoulder, egging him on, encouraging him to take her. The stubborn man took his time, as though he were savoring every second with her.

"You're beautiful." The words seem to tear from him, and then he slowly seated himself inside her, joining them together.

Her heart pulsed full and hard, as Ty dropped his head until his forehead pressed against hers. She wrapped her legs around his waist, pulling him closer.

They started slowly as Ty rocked into her and she arched against him, finding their rhythm. Then their pace started to pick up, becoming more frenzied, more desperate. She was losing all sense of everything except for the two of them as they spiraled higher, reaching for the stars.

She didn't dare look away, didn't want to miss a moment

with him. She wanted it all branded in her brain—the way he looked at her, the feel of his hands on her, the way she felt wrapped around him.

She was so close, her body tense and straining for release. As though sending her need, Ty grazed his hand along her body, now slick with sweat. Reaching between them, he circled her clit as her body bowed higher and higher.

Then the world burst around them, and his name spilled from her lips. A few seconds later, she heard him call her name as he followed closely behind.

Completely spent, she melted against the mattress as Ty collapsed on her, careful of her knee. Then he rolled to his side, gathering her close. She could feel his lips press against her hair, making her feel safe and cherished.

Her hand pressed against his chest, her palm white hot against his skin.

"Wow," Ella murmured after a few minutes. "I—wow."

"I think I could say the same thing." Ty ran the tips of his fingers along her side, lazily tracing a path from her hip to her waist, like he couldn't stop touching her. Up and down, up and down. "I'm not sure if I'm ready to go back to reality."

Reality. She was going to have to face that soon enough. But all she wanted to do was to bask in the afterglow of their lovemaking and the quiet of this room.

Pressing her face against his chest, she breathed him in, memorizing all she could about him. Never had she experienced sex like this. Ty made her feel like she was the only woman in his world. Like she was special. She didn't know if it would last, but at the same, she didn't want to overthink or overanalyze anything. All she wanted was to bask in this moment with Ty and forget about the rest of the world.

THE LIGHT FILTERING into the room was too bright for it to be early morning.

Groaning, Ty pressed his face into the pillow, not quite ready to wake up. The pillow was softer than the ones he normally slept with, and the bed smelled different. Like coconut and flowers.

Like Ella.

Opening his eyes, he looked around the room, taking in Ella's possessions on display—the photos on the wall, the pictures of friends and family, the mismatch of furniture.

A soft white afghan was laid over him, covering his naked body, and he spotted his jeans and shirt in a pile on the floor.

The only thing off was there was no Ella in sight.

A sense of emptiness wove through him as he looked around the tiny room once more to be sure. Ella was definitely not there. At least she hadn't kicked him out of the house, but part of him wondered if she just didn't know how.

He pushed to the edge of the bed and pressed his palms against his eyes. The sex between them had been mind-blowing, and he'd love to do it again. Actually, he'd love to just spend more time with her.

He hoped Ella was on the same page. He wanted to see where they would go.

Pulling on his jeans, he headed down the short hall, taking

in the pictures on the walls and the rugs on the floor. Ella had certainly kept the tiny space warm and comfortable. It was clear she took good care of her home.

Ella was curled up on the couch in an oversized shirt, feet bare, staring out the bay window at her horse and pony. She held a cup of tea in her hand. Her pale green eyes glanced up at him and then back out the bay window.

"Hey," he said softly. The couch cushion sank under his weight as he settled in next to her.

"Do you think the Millers will sell Maverick to me?" she asked, not bothering to look at him.

"I don't see why not. They want him to go to a good home." One bare foot was propped on the couch, and he put his hand on her arch and squeezed. She didn't pull away from him, but she didn't look at him either.

He could see the barrier sliding carefully into place.

"You okay?" he asked.

Ella pressed her lips together before taking a sip of her drink. "I'm fine."

He wasn't taking "fine." "So, in the words of Aerosmith, you're feeling f-ed up, insecure, neurotic, and emotional?"

She turned on him, brows furrowed, and smacked him on the chest. "Hey! That's not fair."

"Nor is brushing me off with 'fine,'" he pointed out. "What's up?"

At least she was making eye contact with him now. And her sassy personality was coming back in full force.

"Don't push me away," he added. "You have a habit of that."

"Stop calling me out on my bull," she grumbled, but he could hear the hint of humor in her voice and her shoulders were no longer tense. He squeezed her foot again before pulling her closer.

"Someone's got to do it." He kissed the top of her head. "You overthinking?"

Ella nodded against his chest. "A little hard to not freak out. You and Jeff were friends for so long."

That made sense. And part of him didn't blame her. The lesson she learned from Jeff sounded like a hard one, and as someone who barely spoke to his mom after she left, he hardly had room to judge.

"We fell out because I realized that he was a complete asshole," he reminded her. "And we fell out before I knew what he did to you. That guy isn't worth our time. Not now. Not ever again."

"I don't want to find myself in a position where I'm just a convenient person to keep a bed warm."

"Ella, you've got to let your guard down at some point. You're going to be alone if you constantly hold people at bay. Do you trust me?"

"I've had Red at your place. Of course I trust you," she replied simply.

A wave of guilt washed over him. He still hadn't told her the timeline for Red's recovery had extended. She hadn't been over the past week, and the subject just hadn't come up.

Now didn't feel like the right time. He had a feeling she was going to take the news hard, and he wanted to wait until she was with Red, so she could see for herself.

Right now, when she was only wearing a tee and looking completely vulnerable, he just wanted her to know that he was committed to whatever it was they were doing.

"Do you want to come over next Friday? You can see Red, and you can join my family for dinner." His voice caught.

His family. The real reason why he didn't want Jace to leave. He was family.

"You don't think that's too soon?" she asked, looking up at him, her green eyes brighter. A small smile played on her lips.

"You just came to trivia with everyone, right? Why not dinner?" It actually sounded like a great idea. A way to show her how committed he was to them.

Her smile grew. "Alright. I'm down. I'd love to spend more time with your family."

Then he could break the news to her about Red. It had to come out eventually, and he couldn't put it off much longer.

His phone rang in his pocket. Shifting on the couch, he pulled the device out, and read his mom's name across the screen.

He hesitated, his thumb hovering as he decided whether or not to answer. If Ella could put herself out there, maybe he could finally answer his mom.

Only he didn't feel ready yet. He just wanted to enjoy the last few moments with Ella before he headed back to his practice to relieve the other vet.

Clearing his throat, he silenced the ringing and set the phone on the arm of the couch.

Ella turned to look back out the bay window, but her fingers were combing through the back of his hair.

"You know what you just said about me letting my guard down?" Her voice was soft and soothing.

"Hmm?" he responded, ducking his head to kiss that delicious soft spot between her neck and jaw.

"The same could be said for you. Maybe you should hear your mom out."

He nibbled on her collarbone until her body became liquid in his arms. "Some other time."

When he didn't have more important things to think about. Like the gorgeous, sexy woman right in front of him.

CHAPTER TWELVE

EVERYTHING WAS GOING well. Swimmingly. Perfect. The sky was bluer, and the fall colors were coming in, and everything felt crisp and wonderful and enchanting.

Yep, as much as Ella hated to admit it, she was becoming one of those women who felt eternally happy. Only she didn't hate it at all. Ty made her happy.

Things felt like they couldn't get any better. The doctor gave her the all-clear to return to her waitressing job starting next week with the promise that she could take her brace off in a couple more weeks; she was still holding the lead in Montana for the barrel racing standings with only one more rodeo left in the season; and, best of all, Ty Hartman was interested in her.

Granted he hadn't stayed the night at her place yet, but he had explained to her that per the requirements of his father's will, he could only be away from the ranch for a limited number of days in order to inherit it during their one-year probation. If either of the brothers stayed away for longer than a month, they would all lose it.

While she understood, there were nights that she wondered what Ty was doing, and a rise of panic would take over. Each time, she'd remind herself they were taking it slow, and just because Ty wasn't staying with her didn't mean he was using her like Jeff. He was over every morning to feed and every afternoon when he was done with work for the day.

For now it was enough.

Which was why she chalked it up to a moment of insanity on Friday morning when she called her father to tell him that Ty was working on Red using pressure point therapy.

"You hired Ty Hartman to do what now?" her father, Jared, asked, his voice a notch louder than before, the disbelief weaving in every word.

"He's working on Red's therapy as she recovers. There's a therapy he'd recommended, and it's supposed to help Red recover at a quicker rate," she explained patiently.

Her dad snorted. "Sounds like new-fangled bullshit to me. Is it actually working, or is he just saying it works?"

Ella rolled her eyes. "Of course it's working. I'm not going to pay for something that isn't successful, and Ty hasn't mentioned any setbacks."

"Because a setback would be bad for him and his business. I guarantee there's something in it for him. Have you asked him?" Jared demanded.

Despite insisting that Ty was doing it for her benefit, and her horse's benefit, her dad flat out refused to accept it.

"You can't trust those Hartmans," he kept repeating.

She gave up after a few minutes. Her dad had clearly hit the point that he wasn't going to listen, even if she took the time to explain why Beau had called in the favor all those years ago. And she definitely didn't bother telling him that she and Ty were seeing each other. She would save that for another day.

With her dad's words ringing in her ears, she hung up the

phone, and chewed her lip. It bothered her that her dad was so against Ty. He didn't deserve her father's opinion of him, just like he hadn't deserved her original perception of him. She knew Ty wasn't using her and Red. If he had anything to gain by working with Red, he would have been up-front about it. Either way, she wasn't going to let one bad conversation with her father ruin her day. Especially when she was looking forward to today's therapy session with Red followed by dinner with Ty and his family.

Later that afternoon, she hummed to herself as she pulled on jeans and a blue plaid button-down. And because she wanted to look nice for Ty, she wove her hair into a French braid and put on a little makeup.

She was looking forward to the therapy session with Red. Based on the timeline Ty had given her a few weeks ago, Red would be just about ready to start strengthening exercises soon, which meant that she'd be back in the saddle before she knew it. She couldn't wait.

Yes, things were looking up.

Hopping into her truck, she headed into town, waving at people she recognized along the way. Funny how something as simple as waving felt awkward, but she was determined to keep putting herself out there. Ty made it look so easy, and she was determined to get comfortable with it.

At first, people looked a little surprised when she waved. Which only made her realize how closed off she had been, but after they waved back, she always felt a little better. A little happier.

As she pulled into downtown, Ella heard an old country

favorite playing on the radio. Raising the volume, she sang along softly as she enjoyed the views of her hometown.

Downtown Garnet Valley always felt romantic in the fall. The two-story wood-framed and brick buildings lining the streets against the backdrop of rugged purplish mountains reaching for the pastel-blue sky always looked so cozy against the leaves turning fall colors.

Ella parked in front of a narrow brick building with a white door, lacy curtains, and a wood sign reading "Cowboy Cakes and Cookies" in script font. There was no way she could go to dinner at the Rocking H empty-handed, and a desert from Stephanie Hernandez's bakery was the way to go.

The red and yellow leaves crunched under her shoes as she made a beeline for the door.

Which would be better? An apple pie or Steph's famous chocolate cake?

Deep in her mental debate, Ella reached for the door handle, when the door swung open.

She leapt out of the way just in time to prevent the door from nailing her in the nose.

"Watch it." The words held a note of condescension, and if the flash of blond hair wasn't a dead giveaway, Ella would have known just by the voice alone.

"Sorry." Ella held the door open, though why she was bothering with niceties when Lindsey would have never gone out of her way to help her in return was beyond her.

Part of her considered releasing the door and heading back to her truck, but after her time with Ty, Ella knew she was above that. She could be the bigger person.

Lindsey froze in the doorway, pink box in hand, as she looked Ella over. As usual, the other woman was dressed to the nines. White jeans, white blouse, gray cardigan, and pink scarf. It was a beautiful outfit, and as usual, Ella felt underdressed compared to Lindsey.

The warm air of the bakery wafted out, carrying with it the smell of coffee and sugary baked goods; however, Lindsey showed no sign of moving. In fact, she looked like she wanted to say something.

"Excuse me," Ella said before Lindsey could slip a word in. The last thing she wanted was to ruin her good mood with a snide comment from Lindsey. Ella pasted on a smile, hoping it would force friendliness into her voice. "You're blocking the door."

Lindsey's face turned a delicate shade of pink and her eyes dropped. "You're off crutches."

"Mmm hmm." She tried to ease past the other woman, but Lindsey remained firmly planted in place.

"You know," Lindsey's voice was smooth as silk, "I have one more rodeo to get ahead of you for Finals."

And there was the snide comment. Ella rolled her eyes but stopped herself from biting back.

The look on the blond woman's face was throwing her off. Lindsey looked…uncertain. Which was something Ella had never seen before.

And that was why Ella swallowed her retort, and instead said, "Good for you, Lindsey. Good luck and all that. Break a leg. Or don't. I can't recommend crutches."

"I—" Lindsey started, but Ella leapt in.

"I'm not dealing with any snide or backhanded comments. I don't know what you have to be jealous of right now, but I don't have time to listen to it." Then, slipping past Lindsey, Ella stepped into the bakery, letting the delicious scent waft around her.

Ella expected Lindsey to follow her in and give her what-for, but the sound of footsteps never followed.

Daring a quick glance behind her, Ella was caught off guard by Lindsey's wide eyes. So wide, they looked too large in her narrow face. Before Ella could ask what was wrong, the other woman turned and left.

Wrapping an arm over her stomach, Ella watched her go. An uneasy feeling pricked through her as an uncomfortable thought rushed to the front of her mind. Had she misread Lindsey like she had misread Ty?

No. She shook her head. Lindsey, out of all the people in town, was the last person she had misread. Granted that whole thing with Jeff hadn't helped. Lindsey had blamed her for Jeff's indiscretion, though Ella tried to explain she was innocent in it. The other woman became nastier with each attempt to clear the air until Ella gave up.

"Hey," Steph greeted her, pulling Ella out of her reverie. "Ignore Lindsey. She hasn't been quite the same since she and Jeff broke up. What can I get you?"

Ella could feel heat rising in her face. Amazing Jeff had managed to keep his cheating under wraps, which was a rare feat for a town this small. Something told her it was because both he and Lindsey didn't want that bit of information getting out.

Guilt seeped through her. While she didn't like Lindsey, she hadn't meant to hurt the other woman.

Steph cleared her throat, giving Ella a quizzical look.

"I'm going to the Rocking H for dinner. I thought I'd bring dessert," Ella explained.

The wide smile on Steph's face lit up the whole room. "Ah, so the rumors are true. Lucky for you, I happen to know that Ty loves the cherry cheesecake. Trust me, bring this, and the man will be a puddle at your feet."

TY CAREFULLY SET out the supplies on the bed of his pickup in preparation to start with ice therapy on Red followed by the pressure point therapy.

He eyed Red's bandaged leg, praying that a miracle would happen, and the leg would be further along in recovery. As it was, while Red was healing well, and faster than he would expect had he followed a typical recovery routine, the mare was still taking longer than he had promised Ella or Jace. And if Ella didn't go to the NFR, there was no way that she was going to talk up this new technique. Hell, she could cut him off at the knees if she was convinced it did nothing for Red.

Ty tapped his thumb against the bed of the truck. He had to break the news to Ella today, but he had to convince her that the process was working. Red's injury was more severe than originally anticipated, and the fact she was this far along in her recovery alone was impressive.

A shadow moved over his supplies, and Ty looked up to see

his brother standing next to him, hands on hips.

"Hey," Jace said, nodding toward the stuff on the truck bed. "Getting ready to do the therapy?"

Ty shifted from one foot to the other. "Yep. Ella should arrive any minute."

His brother tucked his thumbs into his front pockets, the stance resembling one he recognized from Colton and his father, as he looked out over the beautiful fields that surrounded him. Jace looked like he belonged. He wore a new pair of Levi's he must have picked up on his last trip to Bozeman, and the gloves tucked in his back pocket were well worn.

"Look," Jace said, breaking the silence. "I'll talk to Colton about this as well, but I think it would be a good idea to get the property assessed."

Jace may as well have snuck up and struck him from behind.

Stunned, Ty could only stare, his jaw slack.

"I'm sorry, what?" he finally managed.

Jace toed a rock. "I thought it would be good information to have in case the whole make-the-ranch-profitable thing doesn't work out. I don't want to be stuck with a money sink. We have another sevenish months to get this sorted, but that information would help us make a good decision in the end."

"A good decision in the end?" Ty repeated, his voice low and edged with frustration.

"Right," Jace said, as though Ty fully understood.

And while Ty recognized the rationale behind what Jace was saying, the emotional side of him refused to accept it. Despite all he and Colton had done trying to get Jace involved, to see the ranch as his, and his brothers as family, Jace still refused to acknowledge his family or his legacy.

It was complete and utter bullshit. And Ty was sick of it.

"What the hell are you talking about? We're looking at starting a herd." Ty motioned toward the herd of horses. "I have an opportunity to expand my vet practice." He indicated Red. "The ranch will be profitable."

"The point isn't whether or not I'm selling or if we can make the ranch profitable. The point is to figure out the land valuation so that we can have an idea what it would cost for me to sell," Jace said. His blue cap with the local feedstore logo was pulled low, so Ty couldn't see his eyes.

More than anything, Ty wanted to smack that stupid cap off his brother's stubborn head.

"It's business," Jace added, as if that explanation made everything better. As if Jace wasn't talking about leaving behind his family or trying to sell a third of the land that Ty had spent years breaking himself over so they had a legacy they could be proud of.

"Screw business," Ty snapped. He grabbed his hat and threw it in the bed of the truck. "This isn't about business. This is about family. If you leave here, you're abandoning the only brothers you have." His voice choked on the last words. "You're selling the land to spite an asshole who isn't alive anymore. It's a waste of time."

Jace squared his shoulders and shoved his hat back. "I'm not abandoning anyone. Our *father* abandoned me. This has nothing to do with you, and you're making it about you. Our agreement was that if you can make this ranch profitable, then I won't sell my share."

Ty laughed, the sound bitter and harsh to his ears. "It's not like we can snap our fingers and the ranch will suddenly be profitable. This will take years. If I buy you out, I can't establish my practice here. All this work with Red will come to nothing as I'll have to rebuild my savings. You are making me choose between my practice and my ranch."

Of course he would pick the ranch. His entire life was tied up in the land. He could never leave it.

"What is your plan? To sell the ranch and never return?" Ty demanded. That bothered him. Damn it, it bothered him.

Jace didn't answer. He averted his eyes and motioned to the sorrel mare. "What about Red? I thought you were using the horse and Ella to help launch your practice and get more clients."

"That's my plan, damn it." He ran his hand over his face. "The problem is that the horse is taking her sweet time to heal, and she won't be recovered in time for the Finals. The injury was more severe than I had anticipated."

Jace's face grew serious. "It's taking longer than expected? Does Ella know?"

"No." Ty glared at his brother, but the reminder that he needed to tell Ella, and soon, eased some of the fight from him. "I haven't told her yet. I know it will upset her, and I haven't quite figured out how to break it to her. So, for now, can you keep this under your hat?"

"Or what?" The velvety voice was tinged with annoyance.

Oh shit.

Jace's eyes widened as he looked over Ty's shoulder at the

woman behind him.

Ty's frustration at his brother morphed into alarm. His brain began to run through excuses—why he hadn't told her earlier, that this wasn't just for him, he was doing this for Ella, for his brothers, for his ranch. Once he explained, Ella would understand.

Right?

The warning in the back of his head said otherwise as he slowly turned and came face-to-face with Ella.

Her green eyes were bright, her cheeks tinged red, and her brows drew sharply together.

She looked downright furious.

ELLA WANTED TO cry. She clenched her jaw, determined not to cry, and her biceps ached as she clamped her arms over her chest.

Her dad was right.

And she had been so incredibly wrong.

Her body felt tense and rigid, like she was preparing herself for an attack. Or protecting herself from the pain she knew was coming.

"Ella—" Ty stepped closer.

She stepped back, shaking her head vigorously as she maintained the distance between them. She didn't want him near her, and she didn't want to hear his lies or excuses. Once again, she let herself be fooled by a handsome cowboy, and she had fallen for it with eyes wide open.

"Don't even start," she hissed. "I heard you. You were using Red and me for your own gain. How could you hide from me that Red wasn't recovering on time?"

She was shaking. From anger or hurt, she didn't know, but it was better than crying. The crying she would save for later, when she was alone in her shower and no one else could hear.

"I wanted to tell you about Red." Ty ran his hand over his mouth, his eyes wide, as though pleading with her to understand. "I just couldn't find the right time."

"Oh, so you thought it would be better to just get me into bed while I thought you were helping us? Maybe after a couple months, you'd break the news to me, and we'd part ways?" She spat the words out like barbs.

"It wasn't like that. I was planning—"

"To what?" she interrupted, too furious to wait for whatever lame reason he managed to pull out of the air. "To tell me right before I took off for the Final? Or were you waiting to see how far you could take this for your own personal gain?"

She was shouting at this point. Ty braced himself against her words, his hands held out, as though he were fighting her off.

Dropping her arms to her sides, she clenched her fists, feeling tense and dangerous.

"Ella, honey—" he started.

Oh, they were not going there.

"Don't you 'honey' me. I've been through this before, and I'm not going to be placated by some stupid term of endearment. I'm not your 'honey.' I'm not your anything."

Ty's face grew red. "I'm not trying to placate you."

His voice took on that soothing tone she used to find calming, but now it only pissed her off more.

He sighed and ran a hand over his face. "I want to be honest with you. Yes, I had hoped I could use Red's recovery to help expand my practice, but that's not why I was sleeping with you."

Ella cringed. "Right. That was just a bonus, right?"

"No! Not at all. You—" He motioned with his hands, as though trying to find the words. "Ella, I—I've been in love with you for years."

The words seemed to rip from him, as though they were a secret he'd been harboring, and he still wasn't ready to let go of it.

Time seemed to stop, as the scene burned into her brain.

She took in Ty's earnest face, his pleading eyes, the hope that lingered in his gaze.

He may as well have sucker punched her.

Her body caved inward, curling in on itself like paper under a flame, crumpling on the spot. She wrapped her arms around herself, but it was too late.

The punch had landed.

How could he?

If she had meant anything to him, even the tiny little sliver of a bit, he wouldn't have gone that far.

"Don't you dare say that," she whispered. The words felt like sandpaper against her throat.

He reached for her, his expression desperate, but she yanked herself back. She couldn't let him touch her. If she did, she would cave.

"Don't." She looked away, unable to handle the hurt on his face any longer. Her body wanted to arch toward him, to find comfort, to yield to his touch. But she deserved more. More than what Ty was offering her. She needed to cut the emotional ties now and put everything on a professional level, and nothing more.

She cleared her throat. "You can use Red and me as a case to help build your clientele. I'm sure the pressure point therapy is helping with her recovery, and you deserve to reap all the benefits of your work." Ty flinched, but she forced herself to keep going. "But let's not pretend there is more to our relationship than that. You are my vet. I am your client. That's all we have."

It hurt to even get those words out.

Ty was shaking his head vigorously. "That's not true, and you know it. You're scared. You're trying to find a reason not to commit."

"Funny coming from a guy who can't answer calls from his mom or admit to his brother that he wants him to stick around." Ella gritted her teeth. She was done with this. Turning on her heal, she started back to her truck. "I'm going home. I'll call tomorrow to figure out what to do with Red."

For now she needed to get off this damn ranch.

Tomorrow she would feel more sane. Tonight, she'd have the evening to fall apart. She could mourn the loss of Ty and the loss of the NFR. In the morning, she'd pull her broken pieces back together and figure out the best course of action for her horse.

"Please let me explain," Ty tried once more. His voice

sounded as broken as she felt.

Steeling herself against the tears battering against her eyes, she yanked her truck door open and swung into the driver's seat. The stupid pink pastry box was sitting on the passenger seat in the shade.

She had even bought that damn cheesecake for him.

Grabbing the box from the seat, she shoved it into his hands.

"Here, I brought this for dinner tonight. Steph said it was your favorite."

Ty fumbled the box, nearly dropping it before quickly recovering it.

"Ella…" Something in his voice stopped her from slamming the door in his face. The edge of fear, the hint of panic, and something else.

Her fingers froze on the ignition, and she bit her trembling lips. "I can't, Ty. Not right now."

She hurt too much. Even saying his name felt like a slash to an open wound.

"I can explain." He gripped the edge of her door, as though he could keep her there until she listened.

"Did you, or did you not, plan to use Red and me to expand your practice?" she asked, her voice hollow, as she stared straight ahead.

Out of the corner of her eye, she saw Ty nod.

"And did you hide that from me?"

"I didn't—"

"But did you?"

He let out a frustrated growl. "Fine, Ella, believe what you want. Try to make yourself the victim here. I love you, damn it. I've loved you for years, but I can't save you from yourself. Let yourself be lonely, I don't care. Whatever this thing is between us, it's over."

Tears were welling up in her eyes, and if she didn't leave soon, she'd have a breakdown right there in front of Ty.

"No," she said her heart cracking. "It never really started."

CHAPTER THIRTEEN

"ARE YOU SURE this is the best idea?" Jordan looked at Ella, shading her hand over her blue eyes as she squinted against the sun.

It made it harder for Ella to read her friend's expression, but then again, she wasn't ready to face Jordan's hard truth. All she knew was that she had to escape Garnet Valley. For a week at the very least. Longer if necessary. What she needed was some time with her family and a long drive to work through all her pain over Ty.

"It's not like I'm leaving for that long. I need to come back for a doctor's appointment and my horses," Ella pointed out. But there was more to it, and both she and Jordan knew.

It had been three days, and she hadn't heard a word from Ty. She had called him the day after the fight and after talking it out, realized that the best path forward was to leave Red at Ty's place. Word traveled fast in the rodeo circuit, and if it got around that she took Red to another vet mid-recovery, everyone would assume that it was because Ty's therapy wasn't working. She knew it was. After Ty explained the timeline over the phone and the severity of the injury, she did her own research and realized she should count herself lucky that Red was healing as quickly and as well as she was. It just didn't meet the timeline Ty had promised.

Besides, Ty was a capable vet, and she knew that Red would remain in good hands. However, that didn't solve the fact that he hadn't been completely open with her.

Her friend had stayed the night with her the last couple nights, sleeping on the couch while Ella cried herself to sleep. Everything felt like a mess. She was finally getting her life into order, putting herself out there, and falling in love. And in one fell swoop, she watched her love life and her rodeo career come crashing down around her ears.

Jordan grabbed the floral duffel bag that Ella had packed and carried it to the truck. Ella followed with a cooler packed with sandwiches and a couple water bottles.

"Can I say something?" Jordan asked after everything was packed up.

Apparently, she was not going to escape Jordan's opinions or hard truths.

The early morning breeze pushed Ella's hair over her shoulders, and she turned away, not quite able to look at Jordan. "Shoot."

"You're running."

Ella jerked around, staring at her friend in disbelief, but Jordan appeared to be having none of it. Her friend squared off with her, hip cocked, arms over her chest, and a no-nonsense expression on her face.

"I'm not running if I plan to come back," she pointed out.

Jordan let out a snort of disbelief and rolled her eyes. "You know what I'm talking about. You're one of the toughest cowgirls I know. I've watched you fight tooth and nail to get to

the top of the Montana circuit so you can save all your winnings to buy a ranch. And now, just when you get the town to
see you for who you really are—a kick-ass woman who goes
after what she wants—you turn tail and disappear to Oregon
because of a miscommunication?"

"I need some time to get over it," she said, jutting her jaw
forward.

"What about Ty?" Jordan demanded.

She shrugged. "What about him? He used me as a means to
expand his vet practice. He still gets what he wants."

Jordan threw her hands in the air. "Just admit you love
him. I think you have for a long time, and you're afraid to
admit it—to him and to the world. At the first sign of trouble,
you assume the worst because it's safer than trusting that Ty
had your interests at heart. It just so happened to align with his
interests as well." Jordan's arms dropped by her sides. "This
town loves you, whether you are willing to see it or not. And
Ty loves you."

Her heart twisted. Ty had said as much himself, but she
didn't quite trust that it was real.

"This town never loved my parents," she pointed out.

"I wouldn't say that. The Hartmans hired your dad for every roundup and branding. The neighbors cared for you all
through thick and thin. Unfortunately, your dad was really
proud when it came to help and handouts. I think people got
frustrated that your parents weren't willing to turn their lives
around until they almost lost everything." Jordan followed Ella
back to the front porch. "We'd all be sad to see you leave."

Ella flinched at her friend's accurate assessment. Her dad

had been rather proud with handouts. He always believed that things would turn for the better, and they never did. The debt just kept piling up, and it forced him into more and more desperate decisions.

Until he left Montana for a better job with a steady paycheck, and her mom decided that she was willing to work as well.

"I haven't left yet," Ella said.

The corners of Jordan's mouth pulled tight, but she didn't respond.

"What?" Ella asked, then realized Jordan was staring at something over her shoulder.

Turning, Ella spotted a sleek silver truck pulling up just outside her property. The truck glistened under the sunlight, the rims bright and silver, the engine a gentle rumble. It stood out like a tree in the middle of a clearing.

Lindsey Whitmore was at her place.

A knot formed at the base of Ella's neck as Lindsey looked at her and Jordan through the truck's windows.

"What is she doing here?" Jordan demanded, suspicion filling her voice.

Dread washed over her. Why had she started the fight with Lindsey the other day? "We had a bit of a spat the other day at Steph's bakery. I guess she's here to finish the argument?"

"Do you want me to tell her to go away?" Jordan asked under her breath, an edge to her voice.

Lindsey sauntered over, a silver throwaway casserole dish in her hand. The other woman looking completely pulled together. Biting her lip, Ella tugged unconsciously at the sleeves of her favorite, well-worn green plaid shirt she had pulled on over a pair of leggings.

"Let's just see what she's here for." Not wanting to wait around, Ella moved forward, the brace making her movements slow and awkward.

"Hey," Lindsey said. Oversized sunglasses overwhelmed her face, making it hard to read her expression outside of her lips pulled into a tight line. She shoved the foil pan at Ella.

Surprised, Ella accepted it more as a reaction than anything else.

"It's an apple crisp. My mom makes them." Lindsey explained, sticking her hands in her back pockets. She shifted her weight, and then looked around the little property.

Ella's mind flashed back to the apple crisp on her porch a few weeks back. So they finally figured out who made the crisp. That made sense. However, why she was standing there with a second one in her hand wasn't clear in the slightest.

"Okay." The pan was still warm, and her stomach growled at the thought of another warm apple crisp. "I'm about to leave, so I'm not sure if this is the best time."

Lindsey's mouth tightened, and she nodded. "I heard you and Ty broke up, so I figured..."

Nope, she was not dealing with an underhanded gift. Even if that dessert was one of the best things she ever tasted.

Ella shoved the pan back at Lindsey. "I'm not sure what this is for, but I don't need—"

"It's an apology," Lindsey interrupted.

The pan hung in the air, cradled in her hands, between her and Lindsey. The heat of the dessert seeped through her fingers, and her biceps began to complain at the awkward angle she was holding the pan.

Pulling the dish closer to her body, Ella carefully looked Lindsey over, trying to find the crack in the facade. Or the punchline of the joke. Something wasn't right here. Lindsey never apologized. Ever.

"Look," Lindsey sighed, and pushed her perfectly curled hair over her shoulder. "You don't trust me, and I don't blame you. I've been nothing but an ass to you, and for the most part, you didn't deserve it."

"Except for when I slept with Jeff," Ella reminded her. Though she had no idea why she bothered to remind her. It had been ugly when Lindsey found out.

"Don't even remind me. That asshole had been sleeping around for a while, and I only recently found out. You were one of half a dozen." Lindsey waved her hand in the air, as though trying to dismiss the thought. "I thought we were in love. Turns out, he was just in love with himself."

So there were way more than just her. She hadn't realized.

And she completely understood what it was like to be blindsided with the reality that your relationship was built on a facade.

"I'm so sorry," Ella started.

"Don't be," Lindsey said flatly. She pushed up her sunglasses, revealing her hazel eyes. "I should apologize for blaming you."

"I wasn't purposely trying to hurt you," Ella said softly. "I honestly thought you two broke up. That's what he told me."

Lindsey's mouth tightened. "At least you were savvy

enough to ask. I don't think some of the other women knew or cared. And when that came to light, it made me realize that sleeping with Jeff was some sort of revenge against me. What kind of woman was I if these people wanted revenge on me?"

Ella pressed her lips together. Lindsey hadn't exactly been popular in town. Or she was, but not because she had a reputation as a nice person.

Lindsey's shoulders were tense, and the muscles around her mouth tightened. "Anyways, things were tense at the bakery the other day, and I realized that you were reacting to who I used to be and not who I am trying to be. I did some shitty things and hurt you. I know. I don't deserve your forgiveness. I was jealous, and it came out in a bad way."

"Jealous?" Ella stared. Of her? She turned around and looked at her tiny worn-down trailer, her horse and kooky pony, and her old truck and trailer. Not exactly anything to be jealous of.

"Yeah." Lindsey kicked at a rock on the ground. "Your parents were both there for you. You've always been more successful at school and rodeo. And the guys I liked always seemed to like you." She snorted. "Jeff included. I'm not saying it was right, but my dad never paid attention to me, just threw money at me to get me to go away. I got to a point where I was used to being seen only when I was throwing fits or spending money."

Actually, that made a lot of sense. Ella hadn't realized that Lindsey would be insecure. Especially when it seemed like the other woman always got what she wanted.

Lindsey pulled her hands out of her back pockets, facing

them up, palms out. Her eyes were wide, pleading even. "Anyway, I wanted to say I'm sorry, and I hope we can move past everything. I'm not saying we need to be friends, or that you should trust me, but I'd like for us to at least be comfortable around each other."

Ella cleared her throat, the apple crisp still warm in her hands. Maybe she had been wrong about this town. If Lindsey could reach out and try to make amends, she could do the same as well.

Glancing over her shoulder at Jordan, her friend's brows were lowered, but at Ella's silent question, Jordan shrugged, essentially putting the decision back in Ella's hands.

"Look," Ella said turning to the blond woman. "I don't need to leave right away. Do you want to come in and have some of this with us?" She hefted the foil dish.

A small smile broke out on Lindsey's face, and her shoulders relaxed away from her ears. "I never say no to my mom's apple crisp."

THE TRIP TO Idaho was one of the best decisions Ty had ever made. He finally understood why his mom left Montana. She was happy in Idaho, and it was clear she was in a great relationship. Nothing like what he recalled from when she was with his father. Beau wasn't an easy man, and he spent more time pushing everyone away rather than working on his marriage or being a good father. His mom had never smiled much during her marriage to Beau unless she was alone with her sons.

Now she smiled all the time.

She had sounded surprised when he called her out of the blue. Not that he blamed her. He had been climbing the walls wondering about Ella. He hadn't heard from her in days, and when she did message him, it had to do with her horse.

"What else would she message about?" he'd grumbled out loud. Not to apologize or clear the air. Or even to figure out if there was anything left between them. That probably said more than words themselves could—whatever they had was over.

"Maybe you should reach out to her," Colton had said as he walked past Ty's room. "After all, a relationship is a two-way street."

Colton's words had burrowed in his brain, and as much as he hated to admit it, maybe Ella was right. He pushed people away as much as she did. Only he pushed away people close to him. Ella didn't let anyone close to her, but when someone did sneak past her barriers, she seemed to hold on tight. Jordan and Mrs. Thompson and Ms. Minna all proved that.

She hadn't held tight to him because he'd hidden his agenda from her. It had been his fault.

Unfortunately, he didn't know how to fix that. Maybe there wasn't a way to fix it. But he could mend the other fences in his life.

He left Red in the care of the other vet at his practice and went on a two-day trip to Idaho to see his mom. It was his first time off the ranch since his father's will had been read, and the second he turned onto the worn highway and started toward Idaho, he knew it was the right move. He'd been trapped on the ranch for so long, it was the only thing he thought about. It was time to get some perspective.

"This is what you left Montana for?" he had asked his mom as they sat sipping homemade lemonade in the backyard while her husband grilled dinner. His mom and her husband lived on a little plot of land with a ranch-style home and a garden with her two horses and two dogs. It was beautiful, peaceful.

Ella would love it. He wished she could see the place. See that he finally made the effort with his mom.

His heart twisted, and he forced his thoughts away.

His mom nodded. "Hardest decision of my life, but it was necessary. I needed to start over before I was permanently stuck in a rut and couldn't dig my way out." She reached over and squeezed his hand. "Your father wasn't an easy man, and I knew that if I stuck around to keep taking care of him, I'd never get out."

"But you were okay just leaving me with him?" he asked. There was the raw edge of hurt underlying his words.

His mom gave a sad smile and squeezed his hand. "Honey, I didn't leave you. I can't tell you how much it broke my heart to move without you. However, I knew I had to give you a choice. It wouldn't have been easy to finish your senior year in a new town and a new school, and I didn't want you to resent me for it. So I let you choose for yourself what was best for you."

"I wanted you to stay," he said softly. "I thought if I chose Garnet Valley, I'd be enough to sway you."

His mom let out a soft breath and she leaned closer to him, pulling him into a hug. "I had to leave Garnet Valley. I needed the space from Beau, and I had met a wonderful man. For the first time, I realize I had to choose me. It didn't mean I didn't love you or care for you. It had just hit a point where I needed to love and care for myself as well. I finally had to admit that I needed more than I was letting myself have."

"This—" She motioned around her. "This makes me happy."

It was clear as day that she was at peace here. That she loved her home, and her life, and her husband. After seeing her here, there was no way he could ever take that away from her. There was a glow on her face when she smiled, and her eyes were bright and soft.

His mom never looked this happy in Montana.

It killed him that he was angry for so long when it was clear that she had made a choice that was right for her. He made the choice to stay behind, and she loved him enough that she let him stay while also going after what she needed in her life.

Maybe it was time for him to voice what he needed. Both with Jace and with Ella. Either they would say yes and stay in his life, or they would say no and he would move on. Either way, at least he would know.

With that in mind, he drove home the next day. When he arrived home, all he felt was relief and peace. Getting out of the truck, he surveyed the land that surrounded him. His grandfather so many generations ago had started this ranch with hope not only for his future, but for the future of his family as well.

Generations of Hartman blood, sweat, tears, and love was poured into this land, and Ty lived for it. He loved the views of the purple Absaroka range, the endless waves of golden barley and green alfalfa, the livestock that dotted the pastures. The rich smell of fertile land, sweet grain, and mild straw filled his lungs.

One way or another, he'd keep this land, or at least as much of it as he could. The vet practice would come with time. The most important thing right now was to convince his brother that this was a home for him, whether he wanted it or not.

Footsteps on the gravel path that lead to the house broke through his thoughts. Spinning around, Ty spotted Jace coming around the corner.

"Hey." Jace pulled the leather gloves from his hands and tucked them in his back pocket. He wore a pair of new boots. "Have a good trip?"

"Yeah." Ty leaned against the truck, crossing his arms. "Just taking in the views of home. It's always nice to return."

Jace removed the ball cap from his head and leaned against the truck as well. "I've been thinking about what you said the other day. That the ranch has more to do with family than legacy."

He nodded. "It's true. I know this ranch has always meant more to me than it has to Beau or Colton or you. I always saw the decades of our ancestors embedded in this land, and I love the history under our feet and the views that surround us. Our lives are sown in this land. At the same time, I understand why you wouldn't feel that way."

Jace tucked his hands in his pockets. "Truth be told, I've been having a hell of a time reconciling the fact that my father could just up and leave me to start a new family."

Rather than argue, Ty nodded. Jace needed to get this out,

and as his brother, Ty wanted to be there for him.

"It made me feel insignificant," Jace continued. "There were two other sons, and I mattered so little that he never even told you about me."

How could Jace think he wasn't important to him or Colton? Sure, it was a shock to find out they had an older brother, but Jace was one of them.

"You matter," Ty insisted. "You're my brother, and nothing will ever change that. This ranch is as much yours as it is mine. You don't have to stay here. You can sell it, and I will try to buy it. But no matter what your decision is, this ranch will always be part yours. You are family—mine and Colton's. I'd like you to stay on the ranch after the year is up, but if you don't, I'll understand."

There. He'd finally put it out there. It felt a bit scary, especially since he didn't know what to expect from Jace. But he had said his piece, and the only thing he could do was wait for Jace to decide what was best for him.

Jace sighed and shoved his hands in his pockets. He didn't make a move to leave, and neither did Ty. The old cow dog trotted down the path and seeing the two of them, changed course to sit between them.

"It really is beautiful here," Jace said, breaking the silence. He jerked his chin toward a small patch of trees in the distance. "That's our land, right?"

Ty nodded. "Yep. It's part of the original homestead."

"What are the chances of building a little home there? A sustainable one?" Jace asked.

Slowly he faced his brother, his shoulders feeling a little

lighter. "Probably pretty good. I think Colton knows a decent contractor who could help you out."

Jace nodded, his gaze held fast to the trees.

"I think Hailey would like that. She loves this area," Jace said, his voice soft.

"And you? Do you want to stick around?" Ty asked.

He held his breath as he waited for the answer.

Jace nodded. "I'd have to figure out a way to make my aunt move up here. I'm not sure how she'd handle winter, though. I've heard prairie winters are pretty brutal."

Ty chuckled. "Yeah, you're in for a shock if you've never experienced a winter outside of Texas and California."

Jace turned and held out his hand. "Hey, man. I want you to know… You're my brother. No matter what, we're family, right?"

His face felt like it was going to crack, he was grinning so hard. He grabbed Jace's hand. "We're family."

CHAPTER FOURTEEN

Ella drove straight from Oregon, through Garnet Valley and hit the lonely highway to the Rocking H.

It was the end of the day, and Ty should be back at the ranch already.

After the week at her parents', Jordan's words ringing in her head and the conversation with Lindsey fresh on her mind, Ella knew that she had to change a couple things in her life.

One, her father was completely wrong about the Hartmans, and she told him so. It had taken a couple of days to convince him that Beau wasn't wrong to call in the debt. Her father of all people had to understand that desperate times called for desperate measures. After a couple of days, her dad seemed to come to terms with it.

The other? She was in love with Ty. She couldn't deny it any longer, and it was time she stopped running from it. If she could put herself out there for the town, she could try harder for Ty.

She was exhausted and worn after the trip back from Oregon, but she couldn't wait any longer to tell him. The now familiar path to the Rocking H seemed to last forever. Her truck rocked and bumped along the dirt road, and the tiny buildings seemed to be hours away instead of minutes.

At the ranch grew into view, her heart started hammering, somersaulting against her ribs in large, rolling loops. Ty's blue truck was parked in front of the barn, so clearly he was on the ranch. The question was where?

Two seconds later, the screen door opened and slammed shut, followed by the sound of three pairs of boots on a wooden porch.

The blood seemed to rush from her head as she found herself face-to-face with all three Hartman brothers.

She had not imagined confessing her love to Ty in front of his family.

Well, either he wanted her, or he didn't. If she had to say something in front of Colton and Jace as well, so be it.

"Uh, hi," she said lamely as all three men stopped in their tracks. She wiggled her fingers at them, and then grimaced.

Not smooth.

One corner of Colton's mouth quirked up. Jace's gray eyes brightened. And Ty looked like he was experiencing his own personal rain cloud.

"I'll meet up with you guys," he said, not taking his eyes off her.

Thank god.

She watched the two brothers as they waved and headed to the old ranch truck, knowing grins on each of their faces.

"Hi," she offered again after Colton and Jace drove down the dirt road, leaving her with Ty.

Ty moved until he was about a foot from her, arms crossed, shoulders rigid, stance wide. His hat, as usual, was pulled low.

Okay, not a good sign.

"I see you're back from Oregon." No smile. His expression careful, like he didn't want to give anything away.

She hated that she did that to him—made him feel like he had to be on guard around her.

"I'm back. I drove straight here." She tucked her hair behind her ear, her fingers tangling in the long lengths. "I needed some time away and some time to think. And I've come to the conclusion—" She laced her fingers together, suddenly nervous. "That I messed up. I should have trusted you, and I didn't. When I overheard you saying you were using Red as a means to expand your practice, I panicked. My horse wasn't healing on time, my dreams for this year were going down the tubes, all the money I had saved was going to my poor horse, and then finding out that you hadn't been completely open with me just pushed me over the edge."

It felt like her finally perfect world was crumbling down too soon.

Ty's face softened. "I'm sorry I was trying to control the situation."

"I'm sorry that I didn't give you the benefit of the doubt when I should have heard you out," she offered.

"No, I should have been clear from the get-go," Ty said. He pushed his hat back, revealing his clear blue eyes. To her surprise, they were soft and hopeful. "Yes, I had hoped that word would get around that I worked on Red's recovery, and the pressure point therapy would work. Honestly, it is working, but her recouperation was taking more time than I thought it would. I was worried that if I told you Red was taking a while that you would think my idea was bull, and you'd take her away. I wanted the therapy to succeed so you could succeed. Then I could use it as a means to expand my vet practice. I should have told you about my plan to begin with. I never should have hidden it from you."

"I should have taken the time to listen to you the other day," she said wryly, holding out her hands. "I should have trusted you."

"You still left Red with me," Ty said, moving closer. "That meant more to me than anything else you could have done."

"And I told my dad about you," she said. "It wasn't a pretty conversation, but I think he finally understands the predicament your father was in when he called in the debt. After all, my dad knows the pain of scraping by day by day."

"I know," Ty laughed. "Jared called me the other day. Not the easiest discussion I've ever had, but he did apologize."

He was now so close the toes of his boots nearly touched the tips of her worn black sneakers.

"And if it wasn't for you, I never would have met up with my mom or told Jace I wanted him to stay. So you also gave me the wake-up call I needed." The closed-off expression faded into a smile. The corners of his eyes crinkled, and she found herself smiling back.

"I'm so glad to hear that." And whatever happened between them, she was happy to hear that Ty was finally sorting things out with Jace and his mom.

Running her hands down the sides of her jeans, she took a breath. It was now or never. "Ty, I'm sorry I hurt you."

He seemed to melt on the spot, and his blue eyes were focused entirely on her.

"I was so afraid to put myself out there. It was the most vulnerable I've ever been, and I didn't believe you wanted to be with me without an ulterior motive. That's my fault. Not yours. I should have put my fear out there, but I didn't. The thing is, the reason I was so afraid, is because I love you. I've been in love with you for years."

She could hear his sharp intake of breath.

"Say that again?" His words were a soft plea.

Squinting against the afternoon sun, she looked at him and found him smiling. The jittery, nervous butterflies began to fade and became a different fluttery feeling as she stepped closer.

"I'm in love with you." She laughed, suddenly feeling lighter. "I've been in love with you for years and never did anything about it. I just sat around like a fool afraid of how it might hurt me. And it turns out it wasn't you that was hurting me. It was me by hiding myself away." Ella moved closer.

"Are you still afraid?" he asked. He was so close, she could lean in and press herself against him.

She shook her head. "No. Not with you. You've been it for me for as long as I can remember. It just took me a long time to realize that."

Ella reached out, wrapping her fingers around his, squeezing his hand in hers. With her free hand, she reached up onto her tiptoes, her body brushing slowly against his, causing the breath to trap in her lungs, as she swept his hat off his head.

"I want more," she said, her gaze holding his. Her hand circled around his neck, holding his hat so it pressed against his back. "I want you. This last week without you has been horrible. It was only seven days, and I missed you."

He wrapped his hands around her waist. "So you want to give this a go?"

Ella laughed and kissed him full on the lips. "Of course I want to give this a go, cowboy. I'd be a fool to pass you up."

Letting out a laugh that rang happily through her, Ty hauled her close, bent her over his arm, and kissed her.

She yielded to him instantly, kissing him with all her might. This was her man and her partner—the man she wanted to move forward with.

"Do you need to catch up with your brothers?" Ella asked between kisses.

Ty ducked his head and nipped at her jawline before picking her up and carrying her toward the ranch house.

"I'll catch up in a bit. I've been missing you far too much to pass on this opportunity," he said, his eyes hooded as he gazed at her.

"There are plenty more opportunities to come," she promised as Ty pushed the door to the ranch house open and carried her inside.

Six months later

IT WASN'T HER best run, but it might have been just enough to put her at first or second, so Ella wasn't going to complain. The stands were screaming, and the announcer's words made zero sense against the rush of wind that blew past her ears as Ella and Red finished their run in a large circle to slow down.

Waving at the worked-up crowd, Ella exited the arena after their first barrel run of the season. Her face hurt, she was smiling so hard.

"And that, ladies and gents," the announcer called, "puts this Montana cowgirl in first place. What a ride! You'll want to keep your eye on Ella James Sanders for future rodeos. This cowgirl recently recovered from a knee injury and her horse from a tendon sprain. I understand from conversations with the cowgirl that local vet Ty Hartman used a new therapy that was the reason for her horse's successful recovery. We expect to see her performance improve throughout the year…"

Yep, she told everyone she could that Ty was the reason for Red's recovery, and he was getting more calls than he could handle at his vet practice. Some of the top rodeo cowboys had him on call for injuries that needed to be managed. Ty was already planning to move his vet practice to the Rocking H as soon as the ranch renovation was complete.

Red pranced past the gate and to their trailer. Her high-strung horse was fully healed, and despite the bad ending to their rodeo season last year, this one was full of promise.

Ella waved as she passed Lindsey untacking her horse at her super-fancy trailer. The blond waved back. They weren't close friends, but they were on friendly enough terms that it wasn't awkward running into each other.

Red's breaths were still coming in bursts, but her delicate ears pointed back as she listened to Ella's commands. A dog barked in the distance, but Red was nothing but attentive to her rider.

Ella and Ty had spent many hours desensitizing her horse

to honks and barks, and it appeared to have worked.

Someone waved as she rode by, and she waved back easily, not even thinking twice about it as she let herself into the warm-up arena to cool down.

By the time she arrived back at her trailer, the small group from home that had come to support her—Jordan, Jace and Hailey, and Colton and Gus—were gathered around her trailer. Her parents were beaming up at her from their colorful lawn chairs set up in front of her truck.

She looked around but couldn't find Ty.

Huh. He wasn't working this rodeo. Maybe he was off getting food.

"Did you guys catch my run?" Ella asked as she dismounted her horse. When no one responded, she turned to find them all staring at her like they were expecting her to say or do something. "What?"

Right then Red took a couple of steps back, revealing Ty standing in front of her trailer, holding a bright green sign.

"You've got to be joking." She braced her hand on her horse's sweaty neck, trying to steady herself as she read the words scrawled in black ink.

There has never been anyone for me but you. Let me share it with the whole world. Will you marry me?

"Trust me, cowgirl," Ty said, ambling over to grab her hands and kiss her full on the lips. "I'd never joke about this."

"I mean, is this too fast?" Her heart already knew the answer. The man in front of her was it for her. There would never be anyone else.

"I've known you my whole life, and you and your horses

already live on the ranch. Let's make it official, cowgirl." Ty spoke softly so only she could hear. A flash of worry crossed his features. "But if you want to say no—"

"Not on your life," she said, interrupting him and giving him a playful smack on the shoulder. "But I want to see a proper proposal."

Ty smiled, folded the sign in half, and pulled a ring from his pocket.

"I'll take Red and cool her down," Colton said, pulling the horse's reins from her fingers.

Ella barely noticed because Ty was bending down on one knee for the entire rodeo world to see, and even then, it felt like they were the only two people in the world.

"Ella James Sanders—"

"Yes!" she laughed and launched herself at him before he could even get the words out. "Of course I'll marry you."

Epilogue

One year later

"CARE TO JOIN me on the porch?" Ty lifted the small cooler he packed with sandwiches and beer. It was one of his rare days off from his new vet practice and he wanted to take in the warm spring afternoon. "I've got lunch."

"I'm down," Colton said.

"Me too." Jace followed them out the door.

The back porch was large, easily fitting all six chairs with room for more in the future.

"We are breaking ground on the house next week," Jace reported as he grabbed a sandwich out of the cooler along with a bottle of beer.

"Hey, good for you," Ty said, clinking his bottle with his oldest brother's. "Gus says it's going to be a beautiful house. Jones Construction is excited to start on it."

"You'll have us out of your hair before you know it," Jace laughed, clinking his bottle with Ty's.

Ty smiled. He would probably miss Jace and Hailey once they were in their new house nestled by the outcropping of trees in the east field. However, his brother wouldn't be far, and they had already built a new dirt road to tie Jace's place to the main ranch.

Besides, Jace would still be at the ranch every day. After purchasing the stud, the eldest Hartman had taken a keen interest in their brood mare herd. Turns out that starting something from scratch that Jace could build was the perfect way to get Jace invested in the ranch. In fact, Colton was teaching him how to halter break the foals.

"How's the wedding planning going?" Colton asked. He'd proposed to Gus four months ago, and they were busy planning their Christmas wedding that included everyone in Garnet Valley on the guest list.

"Only two months away now," Ty said, positive he was grinning like an idiot. How he got lucky enough to end up with Ella was beyond him, but he'd take it. The feisty cowgirl made him so damn happy.

Overall, things were going well. Colton had settled in at Gus's ranch, which was only a ten-minute drive away, but he spent every day at the Rocking H. He and Gus were talking about building a home on the opposite pasture from Jace just so they could be close by. However, they wanted to focus on getting married first.

"You know," Colton said, taking a sip of his beer. "When the old man forced us to live here a year to inherit the ranch, I thought it was an asshole move; his last chance to control us even from above."

"Yep," Jace and Ty agreed readily.

"But I think he knew what he was doing. Without that one-year period, I never would have fallen in love with Gus, I never would have connected with my brothers, and I never would have moved back to Montana. Maybe the old man knew what he was doing."

"His parting gift," Ty added. Because life at this point was pretty much perfect. Expanding his vet practice turned out to be successful. He had hired two new vets and also started an apprenticeship program. Hartman Veterinary was taking off as a cutting-edge practice with hometown roots that took on all sorts of cases. He also worked closely with the University of Montana to keep abreast of new veterinary methods and technology.

The back door opened, and the old Australian shepherd launched onto the porch, tongue lolling out one side.

"Hey, guys." Hailey walked out the door, belly first, seven months pregnant. "I hope you made sandwiches for us."

Ty pulled out the sandwiches and some chocolate chip cookies. "I have cookies for your sweet tooth as well."

Hailey laughed and kissed his cheek. "You are going to be a great uncle."

"Hey, what about me?" Colton demanded as Gus leaned over to kiss her fiancé hello.

"You'll be a great uncle as well. But you aren't bringing me cookies for lunch."

"Don't forget who made you pancakes with bananas this morning," Colton reminded her.

Hailey laughed and squeezed Colton's hand. "And I loved every bite of them."

"Hi, handsome," Ella said as she followed her soon-to-be sisters-in-law onto the porch and stopped in front of Ty. "You're looking good today."

Ty wrapped his hand around hers and pulled her into his

lap and kissed her hard. "How's the training going?"

Ella ultimately decided to use her savings to build a new barn and arena on the Rocking H property and now had three horses she was training. On top of that, she was getting calls asking if she would consider giving barrel racing clinics. Turns out that once she opened herself up to the town, Garnet Valley welcomed her with open arms.

Her green eyes were bright as she tilted Ty's head up to kiss him. Then pressing her cheek against his, they both looked at the family in front of them.

"How happy are you?" Ella whispered in his ear.

He smiled at the love and happiness that surrounded them, the scene framed by the beautiful Paradise Valley on their home ranch. Soon enough kids would be running at their feet and learning about the legacy they would one day themselves inherit.

What more could he possibly ask for?

"My life could not get any better," he said, pulling Ella down for another kiss.

The End

Want more? Check out Colton and August's story in *The Cowboy's Return*!

Join Tule Publishing's newsletter for more great reads and weekly deals!

If you enjoyed *Cowgirl in Love*, you'll love the other books in…

The Hartman Brothers series

Book 1: *The Best Man's Bride*

Book 2: *The Cowboy's Return*

Book 3: *Cowgirl in Love*

Available now at your favorite online retailer!

About the Author

Jamie Dallas has been creating stories in her head for as long as she can remember. When not writing, she can be found either buried in a book, dreaming about storylines while out on walks, or baking yet again to avoid housework and chores. She lives with her husband and two demanding cats.

Thank you for reading

Cowgirl in Love

If you enjoyed this book, you can find more from all our great authors at TulePublishing.com, or from your favorite online retailer.

TULE
PUBLISHING

Made in the USA
Middletown, DE
31 January 2024

48886603R00154